The Art
of Deception

Liz Harris

A Delicious Selection of Bite Size Reads!

Published 2016 by Choc Lit Limited
Penrose House, Crawley Drive, Camberley, Surrey GU15 2AB, UK
www.choc-lit.com

A CIP catalogue record for this book is available
from the British Library

ISBN: 978-1-78189-359-3

Printed and bound by Clays Ltd

Chapter One

In a matter of minutes Jenny was going to come face to face with one of the men who'd killed her father. Her mouth felt dry, and she ran her tongue around her lips.

The taxi stopped in front of the office block in Holborn. She paid the cab driver, stepped out on to the pavement and walked slowly towards the building, smoothing down the skirt of her suit as she went.

For the last two weeks this was the moment she'd been longing for, and also the moment she'd been dreading – it was almost impossible to believe that it was only fourteen days since her world had turned upside down ...

She'd been leafing through the weekly educational newspaper that she'd borrowed from the staff room. The final pieces of work done by her pupils at her teachers' training placement really did need marking, but getting a job for September was even more urgent than that.

Her heart sank. Once again, the only openings for newly qualified art teachers were miles away in the north of England. That was much too far from Cornwall. Her mother would be alone when she'd gone, and she wanted to be able to come home and see her often, and see her friends, too.

She took a sip of coffee, and turned to the last section of the paper, where vacancies for private tutors were advertised. A few hours a week as a tutor would be better than nothing until she could get a permanent job. Even though she'd worked for two years after leaving school to save enough money to study for her Art degree, her three years at college, plus her year afterwards as a PGCE student, had left her completely broke. She had to earn some money as soon as possible.

She sat up sharply, spilling her coffee. Max Castanien

was advertising for someone to teach art classes throughout the summer in Italy. This was a name she knew well, a name that she and her mother would never forget. She spread the paper flat on the desk and stared hard at the advertisement. Her heart started to race, and she put her hand to her mouth to steady herself.

Then she took a deep breath – she was being silly, letting herself get into a state at the sight of a mere name. There was obviously more than one family in the country with that surname, and there was probably more than one Max Castanien, unusual though the name was. It was highly unlikely that the man advertising was one of the Castanien brothers, Max and Peter, whom she and her mother hated so much.

For several moments, she sat biting her thumbnail, staring at the advertisement. The only other information, apart from the name and brief job description, was an e-mail address.

Could this possibly be the same family, she wondered. She pushed the newspaper aside, pulled her computer towards her and switched it on. It couldn't be that difficult to find out, and she couldn't leave it – she had to know.

The Castanien family had a large textiles company so there were bound to be any number of references to the family and their business on the internet, and if it was *the* Max Castanien, one of the references might say something that linked him to Italy. If the man who was looking to hire an art teacher did turn out to be one of the brothers responsible for her father's death …

She could hardly breathe at the thought.

If she could just meet him, she'd have a chance – albeit a slim chance – of finding out why the brothers had acted as they had done. She'd been twelve when her father died – too young for her mother to feel able to talk to her in depth about it, but not too young to know that the Castaniens had brought misery into their lives. As she'd got older, she'd increasingly wanted to know the reason why.

Her mother had answered any questions she'd asked over the years – but she'd never been able to tell her *why* they'd done it. But with an opportunity like this to meet the brothers, and a chance to find out what had happened for herself …

Jenny felt a sudden surge of hope at the thought of learning why they had let her father down as badly as they had, and she felt a momentary shock at the strength of her feeling. She hadn't realised quite how desperately she wanted answers to her questions.

Several times over the years, she'd thought about writing to them and asking for an explanation, telling them that she needed to know, but she'd always instantly dismissed the idea. There'd be no point: they'd have time to compose something that sounded like a good answer, but which was unlikely to be the whole truth. And if she made an appointment to see them in person and asked them outright – they'd be immediately on the defensive and would probably lie. She'd never know if she could believe them or not.

But if she could get to know them without them realising who she was, then she might have an opportunity to ask them in person. If they became friends, they'd be more likely to want to tell her the truth, whatever that truth was. And even if they lied, she'd know them well enough to be able see it in their body language.

She mentally shook herself. She was letting herself get carried away. The first step was to find out if this was *the* Max Castanien. Her heart thudding with sudden nervousness, she typed his name into Google. As she'd expected, there were several pages of entries. Skimming down the first page, she found an interview that Max Castanien, textiles tycoon, had given recently; she read every word.

When she came to the end of it, she was shaking.

Max answered questions about his role in his local business community, and then, when he'd been asked what he did in his free time, he told the interviewer that he'd just bought a place in Umbria and was planning to offer art classes.

It *was* the same man.

For several moments, she stared at the screen, motionless.

And what about Peter? He was the older brother, if she remembered rightly, so he was probably the guiltier of the two. Was Peter also involved in the art project? She typed in his name.

Seeing the obituaries felt like a blow to the face.

She drew her breath in sharply. Peter had died after a short illness five years ago. She'd been hating him for those five years, and he hadn't even been alive.

Feeling sick to her stomach, she clicked on the first of the obituaries and read it. He'd left a wife and a son of fourteen, Stephen – not a lot older than she'd been when she lost her father. The obituary quoted Max's eulogy, word for word. He had spoken movingly about his brother, praising him as an excellent businessman and as a loving brother, husband and father, and he'd ended up by promising that he would always be a strong presence in the life of his nephew, Stephen.

Peter may well have been all those things, she thought in a sudden wave of bitterness, but he certainly wasn't a good friend. And nor was Max.

She glanced at the small photograph of Peter in the corner of the obituary, clicked on it to make it larger, and stared at it long and hard. He'd been nothing out of the ordinary, she thought – quite attractive, but he had a weak chin.

She closed the obituary and returned to the pages about Max. Further down there was an article about the family business, and as she'd suspected there'd be, there was a photograph of him. She enlarged the photo and studied his face. He was definitely better-looking than Peter, and he had a stronger chin. In fact, she hated to admit it but he was good-looking.

Neither man looked unpleasant, but that just showed

how deceptive appearances could be. A person's actions told the truth, and what the Castaniens had done spoke volumes about them.

But one thing was clear from the photos of the brothers, and that was that she'd been wrong in thinking that Peter would have been the power behind every action that they'd taken. Despite being several years younger, it would have been Max. There was a strength and determination in his face, in the set of his chin and in his eyes, that was lacking in Peter's.

She sank back in her chair, her eyes still on the screen. It felt very strange, seeing their faces after all this time. She could have looked at their photos at any time over the years, but she'd never wanted to. It had been difficult enough to know that they'd destroyed her family; seeing them would have made everything horribly real. But now ... now that there was a chance that she might be able to meet Max in person ...

She sat up. There was no time to waste. She must apply for the job at once, and her letter must be good enough to get her an interview. She glanced at the words of the advertisement again, and wondered how best to begin. She knew that she had enough experience to run his art classes: two years' working before university, her Art degree, and her teaching qualification, and that must come across in her application.

And so must her ability to speak Italian.

Alongside her main subject, she'd also studied Italian. The photos of her work, which all of the teaching trainees had been advised to send in with any job application, would show both her painting ability and her genuine interest in Italy. She'd spent two summer vacations in Florence, looking after children, and she'd be certain to send photos of the best of the paintings she'd done in her free time there. And if she wrote a few lines in Italian at the end of the letter, and included a translation, that would make her application really stand out.

She bent over the computer, her fingers hovering above the keyboard, but her mind was blank and she couldn't move. For several minutes, she stared helplessly at the empty screen, but then she straightened up. It was no good: she felt completely drained and she hadn't a clue how to begin.

Her shoulders ached as if she was carrying a huge weight on them, and she rubbed the back of her neck with her hands. She'd leave the letter until the following day, she decided. By then, she'd feel fresher and less emotionally exhausted by having discovered Max Castanien and by what she was planning to do.

She shut down the laptop, closed the lid and stood up.

The Holborn traffic was loud behind her. She glanced up at the tall office block, and her steps faltered. Everything had happened so quickly. Was she really ready to go through with this?

The day after she'd seen the advertisement, she'd written her letter of application, attached the photos of her work, and had e-mailed everything. She was confident that he'd never recognise her mother's maiden name, the surname they'd used since the newspapers went overboard after the inquest into her father's death. Jenny had felt a stab of guilt about acting in such an underhand way. But there wasn't any alternative. And she was doing this for her mother as well as for herself. She wouldn't tell her mother what she was doing, though. There'd be time enough for that if she was successful. And if she wasn't, she wouldn't have raised her hopes in vain.

Two days later, her teaching mentor at the school pulled her aside and told her that her references had been taken up. Her momentary numbness had been followed by a mixture of excitement and fear.

A few days after that, Max Castanien's assistant, Louisa, had telephoned to ask if she could come up to London for an interview. Apparently, he'd been greatly impressed by her work, Louisa had told her, and by the fact that she spoke Italian. Both things had made her a strong contender for the position.

The gap between the phone call and the interview had passed in a daze.

But she was now in London, and she was about to face him for the first time. She took a step forward, and her heart thumped loudly.

Chapter Two

Louisa gave her an encouraging smile, knocked on Max Castanien's door, opened it and stood aside. Jenny took a deep breath, went through the doorway, and hesitated.

'You'll be fine, I'm sure,' Louisa said. 'Good luck.' And the door closed behind her.

She took a step forward.

Vaguely, she was aware of a tall, dark-haired man getting up and coming round his desk, his hand held out to her.

'Good morning, Miss O'Connor. It's a pleasure to meet you. I'm most grateful to you for making the effort to come to London.'

Her hand was lost in a strong grip, and she found herself staring up into dark brown fathomless eyes.

'N-not at all,' she stammered, her voice seeming to come from somewhere miles away. 'I really want the job, and you obviously wouldn't hire anyone you hadn't met. And you're busier than I am so you couldn't come to me. Not that you'd do so anyway – you're the employer, not me.' She broke off, and went red with embarrassment. 'I'm talking too much, aren't I? It's because I'm nervous.'

He laughed, his eyes crinkling in amusement.

He really is attractive, she thought. The photo she'd seen hadn't come close to doing him justice.

'I suggest we sit down,' he said, and he led the way towards a seating area at the side of the room. 'Louisa's going to bring us in some refreshments, and we can talk. I take it coffee's all right with you? If you'd prefer something else, just say.'

'Coffee would be lovely, thank you. It's very kind of you.' She went and sat on the dark brown leather sofa on the far side of the glass coffee table. Max Castanien took one of the chairs opposite her. The door opened and Louisa came in, carrying a tray. When she'd finished pouring, she left the milk and sugar, a plate of biscuits and the half-empty cafetière on the table, and went out.

'Help yourself to milk and sugar, if you take it,' Max said, picking up his cup. 'I take mine black. Given the amount of coffee I get through in a day, drinking it black isn't a particularly good idea, I know, but that's the way I like it.' He settled back in his seat and smiled encouragingly across the table. 'So, Miss O'Connor, I'm curious to know what first got you interested in art.'

She cleared her throat, and her mind went blank.

Oh, no, she thought in sudden panic. From the moment that she'd seen his name and confirmed that he was one of the hated family, she'd been waiting for this opportunity – she couldn't fluff it now.

She cleared her throat again and tried to keep her shaking voice light. 'It's the classic story, I'm afraid – I had a brilliant art teacher in my first year at secondary school, and she started me off. I wouldn't have used the word inspiring when I was eleven, but that's exactly what she was. She helped me discover a talent for painting, and I haven't looked back since then. And now I'd like to inspire other people in the same way. That's about it, I suppose.'

'That's something we have in common, then: we were both lucky with our teachers. It was a teacher who opened the door to art for me, too. Unfortunately, though, it was the door to art appreciation only – I was beyond help when it came to the drawing side of things. You should have seen some of my efforts.'

She laughed, and she felt her nervousness start to disappear. She pulled herself up sharply. Whilst he was coming across as a very friendly man, from what she'd been told, there was another side to him, and she mustn't let herself be so blinded by his superficial charm, that she forgot about that other side. If she relaxed too much, she might not get a chance to uncover what lay below the surface.

He gave her a broad smile, picked up the plate of biscuits and offered it to her.

'No, thank you.'

He put it back on the table. 'Well, if you change your mind, help yourself.'

'I will, thank you.'

'I'm curious to know why you chose to learn Italian,' he said, sitting back against his chair. 'I'm presuming your family's not Italian.'

She gave an awkward laugh. 'No, and there are no Italians that I know of among my ancestors. It was just that we had to pick two options at college, alongside art. I took the History of Art as one of them, and Italian as the other. I love the work of the Italian Renaissance artists so it seemed a good idea to learn their language, and I'm really glad I did. Thanks to my college, I got a summer job just outside Florence. It was brilliant, and the family asked me to go back again the following year, so I really got to practise my Italian. I've made a point of keeping it up since then.'

'Well done, you. You've obviously got real tenacity. I admire that in a person.'

'What about you? Do you speak any Italian? You've obviously got a place there.'

He gave her a rueful smile. 'I've been trying to learn it, but I don't seem to be making much headway. I could blame it on lack of time, but I think it's more about a lack of flair for languages. I'm a businessman, not a linguist, and I'm afraid that my attempts to speak Italian are rather on a par with my attempts at painting.'

He laughed, and she quickly laughed, too.

He leaned forward and topped up their coffees.

From the expression on his face, she guessed that he was about to say something more serious, and she held her breath in anticipation. If only she'd done enough to get the job. She'd never have another chance like this.

'Look, I don't want to play games, Miss O'Connor,'

he said, putting the cafetière back on the table. 'You were streaks ahead of the other applicants in the quality of your work, and your references are excellent. What's more, you speak the language.'

Her heart was in her mouth.

'Today was about seeing if we'd get on with each other. My house on the estate is only a stone's throw from the one where the classes are going to be held, so I'll be regularly bumping into whoever's teaching them, and that makes it important that we rub along well.'

'Of course,' she said, nodding. She desperately hoped that he couldn't hear the loud thudding of her heart. 'That makes sense.'

'I'm pretty sure that you and I could get on, and the job is yours if you want it,' he said with a smile. A powerful wave of relief surged through her, and she felt weak. 'But don't worry,' he added. 'I'm not expecting an answer this moment. I'm sure you'll want to go away and think about it, talk it over with your family perhaps.'

'I don't need to think about it,' she said quickly. 'From the moment I saw your advert, I've not been able to think about anything other than what a marvellous opportunity it would be. Thank you very much, Mr Castanien. I'd love to run the classes for you.'

His face broke into a broad smile and he reached across the table, his hand outstretched. As she leaned over to shake his hand, all she could see was the two broad shoulders in front of her.

He sat back. 'Now that that's agreed, I can tell you what I've decided. I know I said in the advert that the job was to run art classes throughout the summer, but I've been giving that some thought. My feeling is that it's probably too late now to get a full summer of classes off the ground, especially as I'm short of material that I can use to advertise the courses. I suggest that we treat this as a practice year and run one class only.'

'One class only?' she echoed, her heart sinking.

'Don't look so downcast,' he laughed. 'I still want you there for the whole of the summer. I need you there well ahead of the class so that you can organise everything and order what you need. Then you'll run the course for the week, and when it's over, we'll have a better idea of what to offer in the future, and how to plan it and price it.'

'I suppose that makes sense.'

'I really think it's the best thing to do. I've worked out what to charge for the week this year, but much of it is based on guesswork. When the students have gone home, I'd like you to stay on for the rest of the summer and produce some sketches of the house and area that I can use for promotional purposes. And I was thinking of commissioning a painting of the estate – an original for my collection which could also be used in the marketing material. It would be a real waste not to take advantage of having an artist of your calibre there. So, what do you think of the idea?'

'I think it sounds amazing,' she said, fighting back a rising sense of excitement that she ought not to be feeling – the job was only a means to an end, after all. 'I feel as if I've just been given the dream job: it's the job of a lifetime. Thank you, Mr Castanien.'

'Oh, I think you can call me Max now, don't you? After all, we're going to be working closely with each other this summer.'

She smiled broadly at him. 'And I'm Jenny, of course.' She paused a moment. 'I hope I don't disappoint you.'

He gave her a slow smile. 'I don't think you will, Jenny. I think I've been very lucky to find you. Now, let's talk about dates and how we're going to organise everything.'

Her senses spinning, she walked out of the building.

On the surface Max Castanien was charming, easy to get on with, and had dark good looks and a sense of fun that she'd normally find so attractive; in fact, he was the sort of man you could easily fall in love with. But not her.

She wasn't going to let herself be taken in by what was on the surface. She knew from what her mother had told her that his beauty could only be skin deep. She must never for one minute forget that he was one of the two men whose actions had led to the death of her father. Every time he turned on the charm, she must consciously remind herself of that.

She raised her arm to hail an approaching taxi. If only he were ugly, she thought as she stepped into the taxi; it'd be so much easier to think the worst of him.

Her ticket for Italy and the travel details came soon after her interview, along with a note from Max telling her that he and his nephew, Stephen, would be arriving at their house shortly before the week-long course began. He added that Stephen had said that he'd like to go to some of the classes, but only if she didn't mind. She was fully at liberty to say no if she wanted to.

Of course she didn't mind. On the contrary, she was thrilled: it meant that she was likely to meet her employer more often than she would otherwise have done. The more they met up, the greater the chance of a friendship developing between them, and her best hope of finding out what she needed to know lay in the exchange of casual comments between friends.

She'd promptly written back saying that she'd be delighted if Stephen joined the class. She'd paused a moment, and then added that she was very much looking forward to meeting Max again.

And, indeed, she was.

Chapter Three

The air was filled with the heady aroma of the lilac-coloured wisteria that grew in profusion around the grey stone walls of the Umbrian house.

Jenny paused in the middle of arranging chairs in a semi-circle at the edge of the terrace, and glanced across the garden towards the distant hills, which were shimmering in a haze of blue and purple. Drawn by the view, she left the rest of the chairs where they were, and went along a path flanked by lavender bushes that took her past the pool and out on to an expanse of lush green grass, which ended at the top of a steep slope.

She stood at the edge of the slope and stared at the scene in front of her.

Neat rows of grey-green olive trees lined the sides of the hill as it fell to the wide plain below. Beyond the trees, a violet haze drifted upwards, uncovering fields that were painted in shades of green and sunflower yellow. A road, bordered by scattered oak and elm trees, meandered across the plain to the small Roman town of Bevagna, winding its way past clusters of grey stone houses whose walls and tiled roofs were taking on a golden hue in the rays of the early morning sun.

No wonder Max Castanien had fallen in love with the area, she thought.

A light breeze swept across the side of the mountain and she felt the coarse grass tickle her bare toes. Looking down at her feet, she saw that her sandals were damp where they'd brushed against the dew-tipped poppies and grape hyacinths growing among the grass.

She glanced up and stared again at the view, a wave of sadness sweeping through her. She was about to spend the best part of two months in a stunning place, and she should be looking forward to relaxing and spending a blissful summer doing something she really loved. Instead, she'd have to be constantly on her guard to make sure that the beauty of the place, and the undeniable attractiveness of her boss, didn't distract her from her task, even for a moment. And what's more, she was going to have to put up with another of that hateful family – Max's nephew. It was going to be one long stressful summer, and she almost wished she'd never met Max Castanien.

She mentally shook herself – she mustn't think like that. She'd sought him out and she'd come to Umbria for one purpose alone. That had to be her top priority. No, her only priority. It was the sole reason she was there. The rugged appeal of her boss, the beauty of the place, the thrill of her first paid teaching job – all paled to insignificance next to the goal that had brought her there.

With a last glance at the panorama in front of her, she turned round and walked quickly back to the house. Reaching the terrace, she shook some loose gravel out of her sandals, then she picked up the chair nearest to her and added it to the semi-circle.

'D'you want a hand?' she heard a female voice call.

Looking up, she saw a red-haired girl on the terrace in front of the patio doors. 'It's OK, Clare; I'm fine thanks. But it was nice of you to offer.'

'I don't mind helping, if you want me to,' Clare said, coming towards her.

'It's very kind of you, but I've done it now. It wasn't exactly demanding – a chair for each of the six of you, one for me, a table, an easel and some equipment.'

'There are only five of us,' Clare said. 'At least, there were only five of us at dinner last night, not counting you.'

'There's a sixth, but I don't know whether he's joining us this morning or not. He and his uncle arrived from England late last night. They're in the main house; you can just about see it if you look over there.' She pointed towards the row of tall, dark cypress trees which ran down the side of the garden to the top of the slope. A stone house could be glimpsed through the trees. 'Both of the houses belong to Mr Castanien. His main home's in England, though.'

'Wow, he owns all this? Is he tall, dark and handsome? Forget that – is he married or single? And what about the nephew?'

Jenny pushed a smile to her lips as she arranged the final chair so that it faced the other six. She looked at the arrangement, and moved her chair back a little, increasing the distance between her and the others. Straightening up, her eyes strayed towards the row of cypress trees. He could arrive at any minute – she felt a nervous fluttering in her stomach.

'You can have the uncle. I'll have the nephew,' Clare went on cheerfully.

'Sight unseen?' Jenny said, struggling to inject a playful note into her voice. Her stomach in knots, she went over to her easel and pulled it to the side of her chair so that it faced the semi-circle.

'You bet,' Clare giggled. She rushed forward to help with the easel. 'And it's not completely sight unseen – I've seen the house. Or houses. If this is what they've got here, just imagine what they've got at home. Oh, look; we've got company. It's Paula.'

Jenny's gaze followed Clare's to a woman with long black hair, who was standing under the leafy awning that shaded part of the terrace. The woman looked briefly around her, and then started to walk across to them.

'I hope she's not going to go on all the time like she did last night. She could gush for England,' Clare muttered under her breath.

Jenny gave an involuntary smile of amusement. 'I didn't hear that.' She hooked a large flip-over pad of white paper to the top of the easel and pulled over a low table with a large box on it.

Paula reached them and gave a tinkling laugh. 'So this is where the girls gather.'

'Not by design,' Jenny said with a welcoming smile. 'But we do seem to be the early birds of the group.' She bent down, opened the box and took out a selection of brushes and art paper. Then she straightened up. 'Well, I think that's all the setting up done for now. Have the two of you had breakfast?'

'I have,' Clare said. 'Not that I ever have much of a breakfast. Coffee's all I can ever stomach this soon after waking up.'

'I've eaten, but Howie hadn't quite finished so I left him to it. He won't be long, though. We had our breakfast by ourselves on our private patio. We thought we'd do that each morning, if that's all right. Being newly-weds and all that,' she added, with a little-girl laugh.

'Of course it's all right,' Jenny assured her, smothering her rising irritation with Paula and her simpering. That she was a little too old to be carrying on in the way that she was made it doubly annoying. 'You're all free to have breakfast wherever you want.'

'I'd much rather have company,' Clare said.

'Just wait till you're married,' Paula replied. 'You'll realise then that there's such a thing as too much company at certain times.' She gave another little laugh, pushed her hair behind her ears, closed her eyes and looked up towards the sun. 'It's going to be really hot today.'

'It certainly looks that way: there was a definite heat haze over the valley this morning,' Jenny said. She glanced towards the patio doors. 'I shouldn't think Mr Rayburn and Nicholas will be much longer, and it doesn't sound as if Howard will be. I've put the chairs out, so if you want, you can sit down and wait for them to arrive, or you can go for a stroll round the garden. The view's extraordinary at any time of day, but the morning light creates an almost surreal effect.'

'Good morning, ladies. Or should I say *buon giorno*. We are in Italy, after all.'

Jenny turned and smiled warmly at the grey-haired man approaching them.

'Good morning, Mr Rayburn. I hope you slept well.'

'Indeed, I did, dear lady. Like the proverbial log.'

'That's good. I was just suggesting to Paula and Clare that they might like to have a wander round the garden while we're waiting for everyone to get here.'

'No need.' A tall, slim man in his early thirties hurried out on to the terrace. 'You can tick my name off the list, and Nicholas's too. He'll be out in a minute – he's just finishing his coffee.'

'Are you sure you've had enough to eat, Howie darling?' Paula asked, moving to her husband's side. She clutched his arm and gazed adoringly up at him.

He gave a theatrical groan and rubbed his stomach. 'More than enough, sweetheart. I should have stopped long before I did. You're going to be going home with a very fat husband, if I don't watch it.'

'Then it'll be all the more to love,' she murmured. They smiled into each other's eyes, and their lips lightly touched.

Clare glanced at Jenny and pulled a face.

Running footsteps could be heard from inside the house, and a young man bounded out on to the terrace.

'I hope you haven't all been waiting for me,' he said, panting hard as he reached them.

Jenny heard Clare give a whistle behind her. 'He looks even better in the daylight,' she said in a low voice that only Jenny could have heard.

She smiled inwardly – she was getting the strong impression that Clare's mind that week was not going to be solely on the use of watercolour.

'Not at all, Nicholas,' she said. 'You've all arrived at pretty much the same time. Did you sleep well?'

'Fine, thanks. The bed's dead comfortable. I think I must have been more tired than I realised – I fell asleep the moment I hit the pillow. Or perhaps it was the wine last night. And you can call me Nick, if you want. It's less of a mouthful. I should have said so last night.' His smile was directed at Clare.

'Right, then – Nick it is.' Jenny looked around the group. 'Well, we're all here now, apart from Stephen,

Mr Castanien's nephew, that is. And I don't know if Mr Castanien intends to come across and say hello.'

Anxiety tightened into a knot in the pit of her stomach, and she glanced quickly towards the cypress trees, but there was no sign of anyone. Struggling to get her nervousness under control, she looked back at the group and forced a smile. 'I'm not sure if Stephen's going to join us today, so I suggest we make a start without him. If you'd like to take a seat, I'll begin with a general introduction to watercolour.'

'Who's Mr Castanien when he's at home?' Nick asked, edging round to Clare's side.

'He owns this house, but he and his nephew are in the main house.' Jenny said. 'Stephen's going to come to one or two classes, but it won't affect what we do. If he turns up, that's fine; if he doesn't, he doesn't.'

She sat down facing them, waiting for them to take their places.

A wave of fear shot through her, taking her completely by surprise.

Having got through two demanding secondary school placements during her PGCE year, she'd thought that a class of people who'd chosen to be there would be a doddle and she wouldn't be at all nervous. But amazingly, she felt terrified.

The tension she felt about Max possibly arriving at any moment must be affecting her, she decided. Putting her hand to her mouth, she took a deep breath and tried to quell the butterflies in her stomach. Glancing around the semi-circle, she saw that Mr Rayburn was the only one who hadn't yet sat down. He was looking anxiously at his chair. She began to stand up. 'Can you manage, Mr Rayburn?'

He waved her back. 'Have no fear, Jennifer. I'm perfectly fine. I'm just getting my bearings.' He sat down cautiously. 'I'll soon be giving you young ones a run for your money, you'll see.' He nodded cheerfully at the rest of the group.

They smiled politely back at him.

As she sank back on to her seat again, she noticed that

Nick had managed to get the chair next to Clare's and Clare didn't look at all disappointed about it. She smiled inwardly. He was obviously good-looking enough in Clare's eyes to make her forget about the Castaniens and their houses, which was just as well from what she knew about the family.

Paula was on the other side of Nick, but she had eyes only for Howard, who was next to her. Their every action was punctuated with a loving glance. No surprises there either – they were on their honeymoon, as they'd not tired of telling the group at dinner the evening before.

George Rayburn sat on the other side of Howard, at the end of the row. She noticed that he was surreptitiously shifting his position every few minutes, clearly trying to get more comfortable.

She didn't want to do anything that would have drawn attention to his need for something with greater support, but as soon as they stopped for coffee, she'd see if she could find him a more suitable chair for the week. Whatever he'd said about keeping up with them, it wasn't going to be easy for someone well past retirement age to keep up with people so many years younger, and she must try to anticipate any difficulties he might face.

But that was for the future – it was time for her to begin the first class of the week. And not a minute too soon – she'd feel less shaky once she'd begun. Luckily, it looked like it was going to be just her and the group that day, and that was a huge relief. She'd definitely feel more up to facing her employer when she had at least one session under her belt.

As she felt herself begin to relax, she realised what a strain she'd been under since the moment she'd got up – since she'd first seen Max's name, in fact. But happily she could now make the class her sole focus. They'd paid to be there and that was the very least they deserved.

She took a deep breath and smiled at them all. 'Welcome to a week devoted to painting in watercolour. It's a fascinating medium, and much more demanding than most people think. However, even if you're a complete beginner, you've no need to worry as we're all going to go at our own pace.'

'You're right about it being difficult,' Clare cut in. 'I thought it would be dead easy, but it isn't.'

She threw Clare a sympathetic look. 'I remember you saying in your application that you'd been trying to do some watercolours to hang on the walls of your flat, but had found it very difficult. Hopefully, by the end of the week you'll have some paintings to take back with you.'

'You're going to hang your work on your walls, are you? Oh, how sweet,' Nick said with a grin. Clare blushed. 'No, I think it's really cool,' he added quickly. He threw her an apologetic smile, and she blushed more deeply. This time with a tinge of pleasure, Jenny noted.

'Don't worry, Clare. We'll cover all the points you need to know during the week. Not surprisingly, though, we're going to start with the basic techniques today – the different kinds of paper we can use for watercolour, the brushes, and so on. Then we'll have a short break for coffee, and perhaps you'd like to have a stroll round the garden. When we regroup, I'll demonstrate how to do a quick watercolour sketch.'

'Will we be doing any painting today?' Paula asked.

'If you want to do something on your own, of course you can. You'll have seen from the programme I gave you last night that this afternoon's free, which means you can spend it how you want. And if you remember, I suggested you might like to go into Montefalco later on. It's a lovely little hill-top town, about ten minutes' drive from here. We can park the minibus just outside the old town wall, and from there it's just a short walk up to the *piazza*.'

Out of the corner of her eye, she saw the look of relief that crossed George Rayburn's face.

'I've been here a week already, getting everything ready for you, and getting to know the area a little. The *piazza* in the centre of Montefalco is shaped like a star,' she went on, 'which is unusual as piazzas go, and all of the narrow lanes leading off it have stunning views. It's a place you really ought to visit whilst you're here; if not today, on another day.'

'Are there any shops there?' Paula asked. 'I want to take something back for Howie's mother.'

'Only a few, I'm afraid. And most close in the afternoon for two or three hours. You'd do better to wait till later in the week, Paula.' She smiled around at them all. 'Of course, if you'd prefer to stay here, that's absolutely fine, too. You did a lot of travelling yesterday and you're probably still quite tired.'

'I notice, Jennifer, that you omitted any mention of the red wine for which Montefalco is so well known,' George Rayburn admonished her, waggling his index finger.

She laughed. 'So I did, Mr Rayburn. And I also forgot to mention the internet café. It's on the left, just before you reach the *piazza*. You'll see some chairs and tables on the terrace in front of it. I think it's open today if you want to e-mail anyone at home. It's much cheaper than using your mobile. And there's a car hire place next to the internet café, so if you feel you need to escape before the week is over …'

They all laughed.

'Hey, we've got visitors,' Howard exclaimed, sitting up and staring across the terrace towards the house. 'They must have used the path that links the gardens – we noticed it yesterday when we had a late night stroll. I'll bet one of them is destined for the empty chair.'

Oh, no, she thought, in sudden panic.

She turned to see Max Castanien walking across the grass towards them with a younger man at his side.

Her heart began to thump fast – this was it.

Every single meeting, every single word, was going to count if they were to become friends. And they must. It was the only chance she might ever have of learning the truth about her father's death.

A pounding in her ears, she rose from her seat and went forward to greet the two men.

Chapter Four

'Jenny, this is my nephew, Stephen.' Max Castanien gestured to the young man at his side.

Stephen pushed a lock of light brown hair back from his forehead, beamed at Jenny and stepped forward to shake her hand. She vaguely registered that he had a firm grip, just like his uncle, and that whilst he resembled his father, he had his uncle's square-cut chin. Then she turned to the group.

'I'd like to introduce you to Mr Castanien, who's responsible for the fact that we're here in these lovely surroundings, and to his nephew, Stephen,' she said brightly. 'Stephen's going to come to some of the classes. That's right, isn't it, Stephen?' She turned back and directed a welcoming smile at him.

'Well, sort of. Actually, I was originally going to go to only one or two of the classes, but I've just changed my mind and I think I'd like to do the whole thing, if that's OK with you. I can't draw for toffee, but I think it could be fun.' His eyes were on Clare as he spoke.

'Join the club,' Howard called. 'Just wait till you see how awful I am: I'll make everyone else look brilliant.'

In the laughter that followed, Jenny felt herself unwinding. The worst was over now: she'd met her employer for the second time and it hadn't been too bad. In future she wouldn't get into such a state again.

'Why don't you take the empty chair next to Clare, Stephen? I'll let everyone introduce themselves in their own time.' She turned to Max. 'Would you like to stay for a while? It would be easy enough to pull up a chair for you. I was just about to start running through the basic techniques.'

'That's very kind of you, Jenny. It's an attractive offer, but no, thank you. We didn't get here till late last night and there are a number of things I must do. If you don't mind, though, we'll both come across and join you for dinner this evening.'

'Not at all. It'll be our pleasure.'

He glanced quickly at the group and then back at her. 'Are you sure?' he asked, lowering his voice. 'You're only just beginning to get to know each other, and I wouldn't want to interfere with the group dynamics. Tell me honestly if you'd prefer us not to come. This week you're in charge of what goes on in this house, not me.'

'Please do join us for dinner tonight. Stephen's a member of the group now so it's only right that he joins us if he wants to, and I'm sure that we'd all like to get to know you better.'

'It's very kind of you to say so, even though it's probably not strictly true,' he added with a wry grin. 'But I've one or two reasons for wanting to join you. The main one, obviously, is to have an enjoyable evening in good company, but also I'm curious to know more about the sort of people who come on a course like this. It's research, in a way, as I need to understand the nature of our potential clientele. I obviously had some research done before I decided to launch the course, but you can't beat hearing from people who've actually paid to come to such a class.'

'Naturally. It'll tell you how to focus the marketing next year.'

He nodded, and turned slightly, as if to leave. 'You and I seem to be on the same wavelength, Jenny. As far as Stephen's concerned, however ...' He looked around for Stephen, and his face broke into a broad smile. 'I'm not sure that my nephew's motivation for spending time here is quite the same as mine.'

She followed the direction of his eyes. Stephen was sitting next to Clare, and was gazing at her with puppy-dog longing.

She burst out laughing. 'Whatever your motivations, I look forward to seeing you both this evening.'

And she did.

Her best hope of getting close to the man was most likely to be in the evenings, when he was relaxing after a lovely meal accompanied by good wine and lively conversation. At times like that, tongues were loosened.

Max turned away from her to look towards the group. She glanced at his strong profile, the laughter lines in the corner of his eyes, the suggestion of muscle beneath his T-shirt. If only …

With a sudden jerk, she realised that he was talking to the class.

'… and since I suspect that we're going to be seeing a fair amount of each other this week, perhaps you'd call me Max. There's no need to be formal.' He indicated his jeans and T-shirt. 'I'm not exactly dressed for the office, as you can see.'

He turned back to Jenny and smiled into her face, his dark eyes warm. She caught her breath as a heady sensation ran through her body.

'And now I really must be off, Jenny,' he said. 'Don't forget, if anyone needs anything, tell Maria. It's her job to look after you.'

'I will. Yes, of course.'

'She'll be here daily from before breakfast till after dinner, apart from the afternoons. The others will have to go through you to her as she doesn't speak English, but you've probably found that out by now. But she does understand wild gesticulations,' he added with a laugh. 'That's how I communicate with her and with Carlo. Carlo's her husband, but again, I expect you already know that, and you'll know that he's the one who'll drive the minibus for you.'

'Yes, I do. That'll work out really well, thank you.'

'Right, I'll leave Stephen with you now – he'll come back over when he's ready.'

They both glanced at Stephen at the same moment. He was speaking intently to Clare, his head very close to hers.

'Alternatively, you can kick him out when you've had enough of him,' Max added with a laugh.

'I'm sure that won't be necessary,' she said brightly. 'We'll see you tonight then, Max.'

He nodded. 'We'll come across at about eight, in time for the pre-dinner drink on the terrace.' He gave her a broad smile. 'Well, I'd better leave you to it. I'll see you later.'

He raised his hand in a slight wave, turned and went back across the terrace towards the line of cypress trees.

She stared for a moment at the spot where he'd stood. Then, trembling slightly, she turned back to the group. 'Now where was I?' she said. 'Oh, yes, the basics of watercolour. Yes, that was it. The basics.' Making a determined effort to push all thoughts of Max to the back of her mind, she leaned forward in her chair and began her lesson.

She sat under a parasol outside the small café at the edge of the Piazza del Comune, licking her ice cream while she waited for the class to finish looking around Montefalco and listening to George Rayburn making appreciative noises inside the café as he sampled a variety of red wines.

'It's my intention to take a bottle of the Sagrantino back to England with me, dear lady,' he'd told her as they'd made their way across the *piazza* to the café after saying goodbye to Howard and Paula, who were off to explore the town on their own. 'But before making any purchase, I need to ascertain that the wine I buy is the best of its kind for the price that I wish to pay.'

'Just remember the luggage weight restrictions, Mr Rayburn,' she'd cautioned him. 'And also that you want to enjoy your dinner this evening,' she'd added with a little giggle.

'I can assure you, Jennifer, that I know my own capacity and intend to stay well within it. But I thank you for your concern.' He'd given her a little bow and had led the way past the signs that advertised wine-tasting and into the dimly lit interior of the café.

After she'd explained George's requirements to the vintner, she'd bought herself a vanilla ice cream and had gone and sat outside. As she bit into the sugar cone, she wondered what Max was doing that afternoon. He might be working, or he might have decided to have a swim.

She'd seen a large pool at the side of his house when she'd taken a stroll round the garden one evening not long after she'd arrived, and she could just imagine him streaking through the clear water, the sunlight catching the droplets that fell from his shoulders. It was obvious from the hint of biceps under his T-shirt that morning that he had a fantastic body and most women would find it impossible to keep their hands off him.

A sudden yearning swept through her.

Abruptly she changed her position. What on earth had she been doing, letting herself think about the man like that? She was here to find out the role that his family played in her father's death. Thinking about how sexy he was, a man who'd killed someone … well, she just mustn't. What kind of person would that make her?

A loud 'Bravo!' from within the café broke into her thoughts, and she snapped out of her reverie. Whatever Max was doing that afternoon was up to him. More importantly, George Rayburn was having a good time, and hopefully the others were, too.

Paula and Howard were bound to be enjoying themselves – the two of them alone, wandering around a beautiful little town, surrounded by the scent of flowers and the singing of birds. What more could any honeymooning couple ask for?

It was the other three she wasn't too sure about.

The visit to the Church of San Francesco, which was now a museum, could hardly have been described as an out-and-out success. Whilst Howard, Paula and George had been listening with apparent interest as she'd led them along a sequence of large frescoes, giving the talk she'd prepared about them, Nick, Clare and Stephen had been escaping through the back door. They'd disappeared long before she'd got halfway.

She took another bite of the cone. It was a timely reminder that they weren't students of art history. They were three young people who'd thought that it might be fun to have a week in Italy learning how to use watercolours, but that didn't mean they were automatically going to be interested in medieval art, or in any other sort of art for that matter.

And the same could be said of everyone in the group. Although the Andersons and George had seemed to enjoy the frescoes and paintings that afternoon, she mustn't assume that they'd want to go to a gallery or museum in every town they visited.

This was all part of her learning curve. When she got back to the house, she'd look again at her plans for their visits to Bevagna and Assisi and make sure that she'd got the right balance between activities and free time.

In a way, the present group were guinea pigs, but that didn't mean that they would be short-changed. On the contrary, they'd probably get more than they'd expected, and perhaps more than they'd even wanted. But with the groups next year ...

She stopped short. But there might not be a next year as far as she was concerned. She was there to find out about Max Castanien's role in the death of her father, and once she knew, she'd obviously be off. She and her mother would be able to move on, and all thoughts of the Castanien family would be consigned to the past.

If she was truly honest with herself, she knew that she found Max extremely attractive, and in other circumstances, she'd have wanted to do something about it. But there weren't any other circumstances – and much as her body might be telling her to let nature take its course, her head was telling her that getting involved with a man like Max Castanien would bring her nothing but pain. Even worse, it would be a betrayal of her father.

She felt overwhelmingly bleak.

The sound of laughter reached her across the *piazza* and, looking up from her ice cream, she saw Nick and Clare emerging from one of the lanes. A moment later, Stephen appeared, trailing along behind them. Nick and Clare were the only ones who seemed amused by whatever had been said, she noticed. Stephen looked distinctly miserable as he followed in the tracks of the other two.

A twinge of unease ran through her and she brought her mind sharply back into the present. She didn't like the look of the situation she could see developing between the three of them, and she must keep an eye on them. Two men after the same girl was never good news. It was even worse when one of the men was Max's paying customer, whose enjoyment of the week was a prime consideration, and the other an outsider – but an outsider who just happened to be the boss's nephew.

If Stephen became really unhappy, Max would soon pick up on it, and if he became annoyed by the situation, he might just hold her responsible. If he did that, it would be harder for her to get as close to him as she needed to be. She'd have to do something about the situation if it looked like it was getting out of hand, and fast. But she couldn't imagine what.

'Are we the first to get back?' Nick asked, throwing himself into the chair opposite Jenny. Clare sat down between them. A moment later, Stephen reached them and took the last chair.

'Not quite. Mr Rayburn's inside the café, tasting some of the red wines.'

'Did I hear someone take my name in vain?' George asked, emerging from the café, his cheeks heightened in colour. He beamed around the table. Stephen got up quickly, pulled a chair from the next table into the space between Nick and Clare and helped George into it; then he sat down again. Nick glanced quickly at George, and gave Clare a wry smile. She went pink and looked away. Stephen glared at Nick.

'Did you find a wine that you wanted to buy, Mr Rayburn?' Jenny asked.

'Alas, dear lady, I fear that the Sagrantino may well prove to be beyond my purse, and I will have to go for a good, but somewhat inferior, wine. However, that charming vintner is going to bring in a bottle of a very special Sagrantino for me to taste. I told him that I'd return on Friday, and he understood my assurance that I'd definitely be back at the end of the week. It's quite amazing how the language of *vino rosso* transcends linguistic differences.'

'I'm sure it is,' Nick murmured.

Clare smothered a laugh.

Stephen scowled at Nick. 'Where are the other two – Paula and Howard?' he asked, looking around the *piazza*. 'I haven't seen them since the museum.'

Nick laughed. 'Don't you mean, where's Howie-darling? That woman!'

This time, Clare didn't attempt to hide her amusement. Stephen glanced across at her, and then looked down at the ground.

Jenny felt an increasing irritation with Nick. He was proving to be rather too full of himself, and getting more so with every passing minute. If he continued to poke fun at other members of the group in their absence, she'd have to take him to one side and tell him that it wasn't appropriate. She didn't like the idea of coming on at him in a teacherly sort of way, especially as he wasn't much younger than she was, but there'd be no avoiding it.

As for the Nick and Clare thing, there was really nothing she could do about that at the moment. Much as she'd like to see a smile return to Stephen's face, and much as she didn't want Max to blame her for Stephen's low mood, she couldn't really do more than hope that Clare, who seemed very nice, would begin to get fed up with Nick's behaviour and gradually gravitate towards Stephen.

Initially, she'd tarnished Stephen with the Castanien brush, but he was coming across as very sweet, and in all honesty he couldn't be held responsible for something his father and uncle did when he was very young.

'I've not seen them for a while, either, Stephen,' she replied. 'When we came out of the museum, they went back down the hill. They said that they were going to walk round the perimeter of the town and stop at the churches of each of the eight saints who were born here.'

'Good grief,' Nick exclaimed, exaggerated horror on his face. 'Sooner them than me. What a boring way to spend a honeymoon.'

Stephen stared at him in open dislike. 'So looking at what a town has to offer is boring for you, is it? Well, at least that explains why you suggested leaving the museum when you did. Mind you, you were ready to leave before we'd even gone into the place. Why come out this afternoon if you didn't want to see anything? You might as well have stayed back at the house and gone swimming or read a book. Assuming you're literate, that is.'

'Ouch!' Nick gave a wry laugh. 'There's nothing wrong with not wanting to trawl around church after church, is there? In fact, it's perfectly normal. At our age, anyway. If exploring churches is your bag, Stephen, then you're the oldest nineteen-year-old I've ever met.' He turned to Clare. 'I bet you're no keener on a load of old stones than I am, are you, Clare?'

'So where did the three of you go after you left the museum?' Jenny cut in quickly.

She glanced at George Rayburn and was relieved to see that his head had fallen forward on his chest and he was fast asleep. It wouldn't have been very enjoyable for him, listening to Nick and Stephen having a go at each other at every available opportunity.

'We had a look around the place,' Nick said. 'Then we

went to the internet café and e-mailed home. It's just as well that there were instructions in English on the wall – the man in charge of the café didn't know a word.'

'I said they could use Uncle Max's internet, but they didn't want to.'

'That was a kind offer, Stephen,' she said with a smile, 'but I think they were right to opt for the café. We must try not to disturb your uncle – the accommodation for the art course is totally separate from the main house. Ah, look. There's Howard and Paula.'

They all glanced towards the *piazza* and saw the Andersons hurrying towards them, holding hands.

'I can't wait for the first marital tiff,' Nick muttered under his breath. Clare giggled.

'I do hope we haven't kept you waiting,' Paula simpered with an apologetic smile as they came up to the table. 'Howie and I walked all the way around the outside of the town. It was wonderful, wasn't it, Howie?'

'Yes, it was. But it was hot work. We didn't even stop for an ice cream,' Howard added, exaggerated woe in his voice. 'Would it be OK if we got one now, or are you all dying to get off?'

'Go right ahead. There's plenty of time,' Jenny said. 'The ice cream's delicious. I can vouch for it. I had the vanilla.'

'What about you, Clare? Would you like an ice cream?' Stephen asked, standing up. 'I'm going to get one.'

'Ooh, yes, please; that sounds really nice. Strawberry, if they've got it. If not, I'll have the vanilla, like Jenny.'

'I think I'll have one, too.' Nick got to his feet.

Paula started to lead the way to the door of the café, but then suddenly stopped. 'Silly me,' she said with a giggle. 'I don't know the Italian for ice cream. What is it, Jenny? Howie and I don't know a single word of Italian.'

'I should just stick to *gelato*, which means ice cream, and *per favore*, which means please. That should do the trick,' she laughed. 'Stephen, you'll need *fragola*, strawberry, or you can just point at whatever's pink.'

'OK, then. Off I go. Be prepared for anything, Clare.' Stephen grinned.

Clare smiled warmly up at him. 'Whatever it is, I'm sure it'll hit the spot.'

Chorusing *gelato* and *per favore*, they went into the shop, leaving George, his eyes still closed, Clare and Jenny outside.

Clare jumped up. 'You know, I think I'll go after them. This could be quite amusing.' And she followed the others into the café.

George Rayburn stirred, opened his eyes and looked around him.

'They've gone for an ice cream, Mr Rayburn. Are you tempted to join them? It's a hot afternoon.'

'I am not, dear lady. The pleasure of the wine that I tasted is still with me, and I have no wish to corrupt it.' He paused a moment. 'It's not the easiest of situations, I fear.'

She stared at him in surprise. 'What do you mean?'

'Two men and one young lady. The mathematics don't really work, do they?'

'I thought you were asleep.'

He lightly tapped the side of his nose and smiled. 'It seemed the easiest thing to do. You didn't want to be worrying about what I might be thinking.'

She coloured slightly. 'That was very considerate of you, Mr Rayburn. Thank you. And you're right – I *was* relieved when I thought that you were asleep. I'm going to have to stamp on the situation before it goes any further, but it won't be easy. To be honest, I've no idea what to do.'

'I fear that Nick's a very determined young man, who's not used to heeding the advice of others. But Clare seems a sensible young lady. It wouldn't surprise me if she soon finds our Nick a little too abrasive for her taste. We can but hope so.'

'You're very observant, Mr Rayburn.' She smiled at him. 'In fact, you're quite the dark horse, aren't you?'

'Advanced years do bring with them some advantages,

albeit not that many. You, on the other hand, are very young for such a responsibility. There isn't much that I haven't seen, dear lady, and if I can be of any help at all, at any time, you mustn't hesitate to call upon me.'

'Thank you very much, Mr Rayburn. That's a very kind offer. I hope I don't have to take advantage of it, though.'

'As I say, I think you'll find that Clare will solve the problem for you. She seems a perceptive young woman. But my offer will remain on the table. I believe that's the expression.'

There was a noise in the doorway, and Howard and Paula came out with vanilla ice creams, closely followed by Clare, who held a strawberry cornet. Jenny saw that Stephen had bought the same flavour for himself.

'I see you remembered *fragola*,' she told him, laughing. 'And not once, but twice.'

He smiled shyly, glancing at Clare out of the corner of his eye.

She beamed back at him, and his smile widened.

They decided that they would eat their ice creams whilst they walked slowly back to the minibus, and they set off across the *piazza* with Jenny and George leading the way, and Howard and Paula bringing up the rear.

Halfway down the hill, Clare suddenly called out to the group to stop, as the Andersons weren't behind them any longer. They all turned round and looked back.

Paula and Howard were standing outside the car hire office, next to a pale grey van that was parked up against the wall of the narrow lane. A man in mechanic's overalls was talking to them. Whatever he was saying, Paula didn't look too happy about it, but she glanced at Howard and then nodded agreement. The man spoke again, pointed to the van, made a frustrated gesture and went back into the office.

'That's strange,' Clare said in surprise. 'Didn't Paula say she doesn't speak Italian? She clearly understood what that man was saying. How could she, if she doesn't even know enough Italian to ask for an ice cream? Bit of a weird thing to lie about.'

'We must be mistaken,' Nick said, and started walking down the hill again. 'No one would say they couldn't speak Italian if they could. There'd be no reason to lie about it. In fact, they're more likely to say that they can speak the lingo when they can't, rather than the other way round.'

'Could you hear what they were saying?' Stephen asked.

'Not really. We were too far away,' Clare replied.

'Well, that's it, then.' Nick smiled in triumph. 'The computer instructions were in English, weren't they? And so were the details on the wall outside the car hire office. We know the man in the internet café doesn't speak English, so I bet it's the car hire man who does.'

Stephen nodded in agreement. 'What Nick says makes sense, Clare.'

Clare's face cleared. 'You're right, it does.'

A moment later, Paula came clattering behind them on the cobblestones.

Chapter Five

Jenny lingered beneath a mulberry tree at the side of the terrace and watched them.

Max was standing at the edge of the terrace, looking cool and relaxed in well-cut chinos and a pale grey open-necked shirt. He had a glass in his hand and was staring out at the garden. Stephen hovered at his side, clearly restless, his back to the view, his eyes riveted to the patio doors. Every so often, Max looked around at Stephen and said something to him. Each time, though, he had to nudge Stephen and repeat himself before Stephen was able to answer him.

It was pretty clear what Stephen was thinking about.

But it wasn't so easy to know what went on inside his uncle's mind, she thought.

Max came across as open and uncomplicated, but no matter how genuine he seemed, it must all be a veneer. Unfortunately for her, it was a veneer that seemed to be firmly in place. From the small amount she'd seen of him, she knew that it wasn't going to be easy to discover what lurked beneath the easy charm.

And she didn't have unlimited time, which made it all the more difficult.

As far as she knew, he was only going to be joining them in the evenings. It was true that when the end of the week arrived, all the members of the class would go home and she'd be alone for the rest of the summer, doing the paintings that he wanted, but he might decide to leave for England soon after the others. If he did, she wouldn't have had sufficient time to find out why he and his brother had behaved so cruelly towards her father, and that meant the part that they'd played in his death could forever remain a mystery.

Of course, she might always have another chance the following summer, but there was no guarantee that Max would want to see art classes there again, much as he might think now that he would. And even if he did, there was no certainty he'd ask her to run them for him.

If he did … the thought of waiting another whole year before she could try to find out the truth … well, it didn't bear thinking about.

She'd have to take advantage of every opportunity she was offered, no matter how slight, to encourage him to stay on in Italy for at least some of the time that she'd be there on her own. If he did so, she'd see him occasionally and she'd have to make the most of that time.

They'd probably not get much beyond exchanging platitudes and discussing her drawings. There wasn't enough time to build more of a friendship than that, but exchanging platitudes would be better than nothing, and might just lead to something more. It was vital that she worked on their friendship in the few evenings that they had together that week, and she couldn't afford to waste a single precious minute.

The patio doors suddenly swung open and Clare came through them, wearing a short yellow cotton dress, her hair a mass of lustrous red curls that gleamed in the light. Nick followed closely behind her.

Stephen made a beeline for Clare. 'Can I get you a drink?' he asked, positioning himself in front of her.

'Ooh, yes, please.'

He went over to the table at the side of the terrace, where several bottles of Prosecco lay on a bed of ice alongside a glass jug of peach purée, picked up one of the bottles and opened it. When he'd finished mixing two Bellinis, he carried one of the drinks carefully across to Clare.

Jenny moved swiftly to the table and helped herself to the other drink. Raising her glass to Stephen, she laughingly thanked him as she hurried across the terrace to Max's side.

Max glanced down at her, smiled briefly, then looked back at the view. She followed his gaze across the spotlit garden to the feathery tips of the olive trees, their fragile leaves a deepening grey in the fading light of the day.

'This is truly an artist's paradise, Max. The view from up here is inspirational.'

'It is, isn't it? It looks different in every light, but with the sun setting over the plain, this is a particularly beautiful time of day. It's my favourite, in fact.'

'I think it's mine, too,' she said. 'It's so calm. But a place like this always holds something for an artist, no matter the time.'

'You're absolutely right about that. I don't remember if I told you in London, but I collect paintings in a small way – nothing terribly grand – and whilst I obviously enjoy looking at my pictures, nothing surpasses the pleasure I get from a view like this. There's always something new to be discovered.'

'I'm guessing that there's a connection between your fondness for your art collection and the fact that you've set up the courses here.'

'I'm sure that's true, but it also owes a lot to my total lack of artistic skill. I really admire anyone who can paint – perhaps because I'm so useless at it myself – and if I can do anything at all to help those interested in art to improve, then so be it.'

Jenny gave him a sly smile. 'And of course, it's nothing to do with the profitable use of pre-existing facilities.'

Max laughed. 'Well, maybe just a little bit. I am a businessman, after all. But it's a bit of a worry, you being able to read me like a book,' he added in amusement.

'Perhaps "like a painting" would be a better comparison in the circumstances,' she said with a smile. She tore her eyes away from his face, and forced them back to the view ahead of her. 'Whatever the reason, it's a wonderful place to have an art course and I'm glad that you decided to go down this path.'

'Me, too. But you wouldn't believe how many people were against it.'

'Against it?' She turned to him in surprise. 'Why on earth would they be against it? It's a brilliant idea.'

'You should put on cookery courses, I was told by anyone I mentioned my plans to. It's the in thing. But imagine being indoors all day, tied to a hot stove, peeling potatoes, chopping vegetables, when there's all this going on in the world outside.' He gestured to the garden. 'Nope, I told them, it's got to be art classes.'

Who had he discussed his plans with, she wondered and took a sip of her drink. She was pretty sure he wasn't married. There hadn't been any mention of a wife in the articles she'd read online. But there could be a girlfriend back in England, and, thinking about it, there probably was. The fact that he ran a successful company and had property abroad was more than enough to make him highly eligible.

She glanced up at his strong profile, and a sudden heat rushed to her face.

And so was the fact that he was very, very good-looking. Even if he didn't have a single penny to his name, he would still have been in great demand.

But not by her. Even if she wanted to fall for him, her feelings about what had happened to her father would stop that happening.

Also, she was in danger of assuming that because she found him so attractive, he might want something more from her, too. But there was no reason to think that just because he'd offered her a job he'd start to look at her in a romantic way. And if he didn't, it'd be so much easier for her to keep her focus.

A thought suddenly hit her, and she felt a sharp stab of panic. If he *did* have a girlfriend, she might be planning to join him at some point over the summer. It wasn't something he would have mentioned at the interview in London – his plans for the summer were none of her business – but just in case a girlfriend *was* coming out, it was all the more urgent that she develop a friendship with him as quickly as possible.

Inspiration struck.

'You're right,' she said with a bright smile. 'Art classes are much more suitable for this location than cookery would have been. But you're wrong about something you said earlier, or rather you're wrong about something you implied.'

He looked at her in surprise. 'What do you mean?'

'You said that you didn't have any ability for art.'

'Well, I haven't – I'm absolutely hopeless at drawing and painting, and trust me that's an understatement.'

'But you could learn to paint. It's a myth that you've either got talent or you haven't – everyone can be taught. After that, it's just hard work.'

'Do you really believe that?'

'I know it's true. I've seen people start an art class without a clue which end of the brush to hold. And I've watched them work hard, lesson after lesson, until in the end they're absolutely amazed at what they've achieved.'

'Thinking of my past efforts, I find that virtually impossible to believe,' he said with a wry smile. 'I'm afraid I'm still inclined to subscribe to the natural ability theory: I'm the living proof of that.'

'So put it to the test,' she said lightly, trying not to show how much she wanted him to agree. 'Come along to some of my classes and see how you get on. Stephen's going to join us; you could come over with him. There's more than enough equipment for an extra artist.'

She held her breath.

'I might just do that,' he said slowly. 'You've got me thinking now. It could be fun, and after all, what have I got to lose? You know, you may just have got yourself another pupil.'

She let her breath out slowly. If Max came to the classes, she'd see a lot more of him. It was a start, but no more than that, as the others would be there, too. She must keep on thinking. What she really needed was quality time alone with him, which meant she'd have to come up with a way of getting him by himself.

She glanced at him, at the planes of his face, which gleamed like burnished gold in the rays thrown out by the dying sun.

Her mind went into overdrive. Then, bingo – inspiration struck again. She had an idea, and if she got it right, Max might pick up the threads and make the suggestion she wanted …

'You know you ignored all advice and chose art over cookery,' she said, injecting a bouncing lilt into her voice, 'for purely selfish reasons, I'm very glad you did.'

'For selfish reasons? Now that's intriguing.' He looked amused, she was pleased to see.

'Yes, definitely for selfish reasons. I wouldn't be here if you'd plumped for cookery, would I? I make a mean omelette, but I'd be hard pushed to stretch that skill for a whole week. Day one, find bowl; day two, remove three eggs from beneath nearest chicken; day three, break said eggs into bowl. And so on.'

He laughed. 'You've got a point there. Yes, I think I might have expected a little more for my money, both as an employer and as a punter. Now, if you'd been able to make *tagliatelle al tartufo*, in addition to making an omelette, then we could have been in business.'

A bolt of excitement shot through her. She could build on this. 'That's your favourite dish, is it?'

'Indeed it is.'

She sighed loudly. 'Sadly, that's not in my repertoire: truffles don't abound in Cornwall and the family I was with in Florence never had them. At least, not the truffly kind: only the chocolate sort.' She let a trace of innocent flirtation creep into her voice. 'That means I'd have been handicapped from the start. I'd never be able to master something I've not even tasted. I wouldn't know what I was aiming for.'

He caught his breath in mock horror and raised his hand.

'We need to fix that, and fast, just in case I ever decide

to give in and replace art with cookery. We'll look at the activities you've planned for the coming week, and pick a day when the class will be so worn out by the evening that they won't notice if you sneak off and play hooky. Then you and I can go to a place I know in Bevagna that serves the best Umbrian food.'

Success! She'd done it.

But she must watch what she said, she thought quickly. Sounding too eager could be counterproductive with a man who was probably bored rigid by women throwing themselves at him, and she wouldn't want him to think her interest in him was anything more than simple friendship.

'That's very kind of you, Max, but you don't have to, you know. I could order it when we go to Assisi. We're there for the whole of Wednesday.' Smiling, she glanced up at him, and caught him staring intently down at her. Their eyes met.

'No, I prefer my plan,' he said with a slight smile, and he turned back to the garden. '*Tagliatelle al tartufo* is something to be tasted for the first time when you're with a connoisseur. And apart from that, after the amount of time I've spent with Stephen recently, I'd quite enjoy a change of company.'

His final words were almost drowned out by the sound of Clare screaming with laughter. They turned at the same moment to see what was happening.

Stephen had opened a new bottle of Prosecco and the sparkling wine had gone all over his hands. To Clare's amusement, he was licking the wine off his skin.

'I rest my case,' Max said with a grin.

Laughter lines crinkled the corners of his eyes whenever he smiled, she noticed. And that was often. And he had the deepest brown eyes she'd ever seen.

Dragging her eyes away from Max, she caught sight of Nick, who was standing just behind Clare, watching Stephen with a supercilious air. She felt a momentary chill, and her eyes moved to Stephen. She smiled vaguely in his direction. 'Stephen seems nice,' she said, watching him pour the remaining Prosecco into Clare's glass.

Max glanced at his nephew. 'Yes, he's a really great kid and I'm very fond of him, but there are limits to how much one wants to hear about the million and one forms of social networking that he enjoys, and about his music and so on. Nope, I'm ready for a more adult sort of conversation. Having dinner with the group tonight will be a good start – at least, I hope it will be – and we can get to know each other even better if you'll have dinner with me one evening this week.'

A warm glow crept through her. She couldn't have asked for a more successful outcome to their conversation. For a moment, she imagined them sitting opposite each other at a small table, a candle flickering between them …

She kicked herself back into the present.

'I hope you *do* enjoy this evening,' she said quickly. 'They're a mixed bunch, and some are more adult than others. I'm sure there are also some bores you wouldn't want to sit next to.' She smiled at him. 'For your sake, I hope the conversation this evening will be on the more adult side, rather than less.'

'Adult or not, I'm grateful to you for letting me barge into what is, after all, your show.'

'I prefer to think of it as *our* show.'

He raised his hands in surrender. 'OK. I'll go along with it being a joint thing. And now, in the interests of adult conversation, I think I'd better try to inject some maturity into Stephen before we sit down for dinner. Excuse me, would you?'

As he went across to Stephen, Paula and Howard came on to the terrace, arm in arm.

'This is going to be the perfect end to what has been a simply perfect day,' Paula trilled to no one in particular. She smoothed down the skirt of her dress – a profusion of brightly coloured flowers on a white background – adjusted the flower in her hair, pulled her shawl around her shoulders and gazed up at the leafy awning. 'Oh, look, Howie. Aren't those fairy lights adorable? So atmospheric. This really is the most wonderful honeymoon.'

He slid his arm around her, pulled her to him and kissed her cheek.

'Yuk,' Jenny heard Nick mutter. 'I think I'm going to throw up. And that dress – she looks like she should be in a vase.'

Stephen glanced at Nick, and moved from Clare's side to the Prosecco table. 'We're having Bellinis this evening,' he called to Howard and Paula. 'Can I make you one? It's the real thing, peach purée and all that.'

'Sounds good to me,' Howard said. 'We'll both have one, thanks. And Mr Rayburn's on his way, too. We overtook him while he was looking at one of the paintings. You could pour one for him while you're at it.'

'No sooner said than done.' Stephen arranged three glasses in a row, spooned a little peach purée into each and picked up the bottle of Prosecco.

'Nice dress, Paula,' Clare said politely.

'I'm glad you like it. It's Howie's favourite,' Paula said, visibly preening at the compliment.

Stephen finished pouring the wine and was carrying two glasses over to the Andersons as George Rayburn wandered out on to the terrace. Jenny went over to him at once.

'Good evening, Mr Rayburn. I hope you were able to get some rest after today's exertions.'

'Indeed, I was, thank you. I sat in the shade just outside my room, and before I knew it, it was way past the time that I should have been here. I do apologise.'

'Don't think twice about it. This is a holiday as well as a class. Your sleep will have done you the world of good, and you'll enjoy the evening all the more for it. Now, I think Stephen's made you a drink. We're having Bellinis, but if you'd prefer something else, you only have to say.'

'No, I'm sure that it will be delicious.' He took a glass

from Stephen. 'Thank you, dear boy. Don't you worry about me, Jennifer. I shall go and talk to Paula and Howard. I've just been looking at the painting that I saw them studying earlier today. It really is a most interesting picture and I look forward to hearing what they thought of it.'

As George walked across to the Andersons, Jenny turned and strolled back to Max, who was standing alone now. 'Well, that's all of us here now,' she told him. 'As I said, we're a mixed bunch.'

'Mixed or not, everyone seems to be very pleased with everything, with maybe one exception.' He indicated Nick. 'But I think that's more to do with the girl than with anything else. She seems very pleasant, not to mention pretty, and it's hardly surprising that both young men are smitten. No, you've obviously made everyone feel at ease, and very quickly, too. As I believe I've said before, I was lucky to find you.'

'I'd say that I'm the one who's lucky,' she said, smiling up into his face. 'I had to find a job for the summer, and this is way beyond my wildest dreams.'

She was indeed the lucky one, she thought, being given the chance to finally discover what happened to her father.

'I think we'll have to agree that we're both lucky,' he said warmly, and she noticed that his eyes lingered on her face. 'So, what did you do this morning after I left Stephen with you?'

'I showed them how to do a quick watercolour sketch. By the way, I'm keeping all the drawings I do for you to see at the end of the week. Obviously, everyone will take the paintings home that they want to keep, but they might leave some of their work behind. Between what's left here and what I do in the week, we should have plenty to use in the advertising.'

'Sounds good to me.' He looked across in Stephen's direction and smiled. 'I'm very keen to see how Stephen gets on. You've certainly got your work cut out with him.'

He glanced sideways at her. 'And with me, too, if I do decide to come to a few classes. I must confess I'm quite tempted.'

She opened her mouth to urge him to yield to temptation, but Maria appeared at the patio doors.

'*La cena è pronta*,' she announced.

'Dinner is ready,' Jenny translated. She smiled round at the group. 'Shall we go and see what's waiting for us?'

Chapter Six

Jenny sat back in her chair, cupping her mug of coffee. She glanced round at the empty table, and felt very pleased with herself – she was the only person who'd stayed behind on the terrace after lunch. Everyone else, including Max, had gone back to the part of the house or garden that they were painting.

She'd set them the task of practising how to mix watercolour with pastel and coloured pencil, something she'd demonstrated that morning. They'd had time to start practising before the end of the morning, and she was thrilled that they were all so keen to get going again.

And she was also very relieved that she'd persuaded Maria to serve a lunch that was more in keeping with the eating habits of the British than the Italians. When Maria had come to her that morning and suggested an Italian-style lunch of *antipasti* followed by two pasta dishes, one after the other, and ending with *tiramisù*, she'd had a horrible vision of the whole class finishing their lunch and taking to their beds for a never-ending afternoon siesta.

Using all of her tact, she'd got Maria to scale down the lunch to a comparatively modest *prosciutto* with melon, followed by a dish of *farfalle* pasta lightly tossed in a basil pesto, accompanied by a classic Orvieto white wine, and finally a large yellow peach, some pecarino cheese and coffee. It had proved to be ideal – delicious, but not so heavy that it dulled their enthusiasm for the afternoon's activity.

She glanced at her watch. They would have started on their work by now. She'd let them have a little longer, and then go and see how they were getting on. She'd leave Paula and Howard's work till last as she'd seen their drawings that morning, and she'd give George's work a miss for the same reason.

Finding out what each of the group had chosen to paint

was going to be one of the most interesting parts of the week. Their choice of location spoke volumes about their character and interests, and, to a certain extent, about their ability.

She was particularly interested in seeing what Max had chosen to draw.

It was so hard to know what to make of him.

If it hadn't been for what her mother had repeatedly told her about him and Peter, she would have taken him at face value. He came across as a man without guile, charming, easy-going, ready to be pleased – a man whose business success hadn't gone to his head in any way. Under different circumstances, he was a man she could easily have fallen in love with.

But her mother's words were always there, burning away in the back of her mind, stopping her from being taken in by his attractive exterior, forcing her to keep an emotional distance.

Unsurprisingly, she wasn't the only person who found Max to be excellent company. Several of the group had initially been less than keen on him joining them for dinner – Nick for example, and even Clare, although she'd been less vocal about it. But George had seemed delighted at the prospect of Max's company, and Howard and Paula even more so. In fact, she'd been amazed at how enthusiastic the Andersons had been about Max joining them, given that they always seemed so complete in themselves and had never appeared particularly eager to join the others.

However, any reservations about him joining them, and any fears that conversation might be awkward in the presence of the man who owned the property, had clearly been swept away the night before. Even Nick had visibly been won over.

Furthermore, if any doubts had lingered overnight and resurfaced in the morning, they would have been instantly wiped away at the sight of Max rolling up with Stephen after breakfast, carrying an easel and watercolours.

'I thought I'd better not miss any more lessons,' he'd told them, and she'd seen from their faces how pleased they were that he'd enjoyed their company so much that he'd come back for more.

He'd placed his chair and easel next to George, sat down and smiled round at them all. As he'd completed his visual tour of the group, she couldn't help being aware of his eyes on her. She'd felt hot under his gaze. Her stomach had fluttered, and for a moment or two she'd felt disorientated.

But she'd pulled herself together – she'd had to – and, trying to avoid looking at him more than she needed to, she'd begun to demonstrate the art of painting landscapes. Gradually, she'd settled down, and she'd felt quite relaxed by the time it came to showing them the different ways of applying watercolour and how to mix it with other media. After that, they'd spread out in the garden and begun to work on their own sketches. She'd given them time to make a good start on their basic outline, and had then gone from one to the other, looking at each picture and making constructive suggestions.

As soon as she'd reached Paula, she'd stopped and stared at her drawing in amazement.

If she'd had to predict that one of the group would be flowery and superficial, that person would have been Paula. And she would have been completely wrong. Instead of a pretty little confection that bore no relationship at all to the object she was painting, Paula's work revealed her to be a true artist.

'If you decided to take art really seriously, Paula,' she had told her, 'you could be very good. You have real talent.'

Paula had blushed and simpered. 'Oh, no, I couldn't – could I, Howie?'

She'd felt a sharp irritation with a woman who clearly had ability, but who couldn't decide upon anything without first checking with her husband. Before she said anything rude, she'd swiftly moved on to Howard.

Whatever he'd earlier said about his work being rubbish,

his picture, too, showed above average skill. But whilst it was technically good, it was more pedestrian than Paula's and it lacked the indefinable quality that she'd glimpsed in Paula's work.

'Both of you are very good,' she'd told them. 'Is this the first art course that you've been on?'

'We did art at school – that's where we met,' Howard had said. 'We went our separate ways afterwards, but happily our paths crossed a few years later, and the rest is history,' He'd smiled affectionately at Paula and turned back to his painting.

'You must have had an excellent teacher,' she remarked. 'I look forward to seeing the rest of the painting you do this week.' And she moved away to look at George's work.

If Paula and Howard's technical ability was at one end of the spectrum, George's was at the other. Despite clearly making a great effort, he couldn't draw and he didn't have a natural feeling for the medium.

He'd glanced up at her as she'd been studying his work, trying hard to find something to praise.

'Trouble yourself not, Jennifer,' he'd said with a sigh. 'Not even this comfortable chair, which you have been so kind as to find for me, can help. I'm under no illusions about my skill, or rather my lack of skill, so you may cease your mental strain and express an honest opinion.'

She'd laughed. 'You're too hard on yourself, Mr Rayburn.'

'And you are too kind, dear lady. Watercolours were my wife's passion. Our home is full of them. Sadly, though, I doubt that I shall be adding to our collection with a creation of my own: the talent of the many artists who've captured life in watercolour seems to have quite passed me by.'

'Your wife?'

'Agnes. She passed away a few months ago. It had been her dream to come on a course like this. Indeed, we'd found the details of this course before she died and we'd already started to plan our trip. Unfortunately, it was not to be. I decided, however, to do the course for both of us. It's what Agnes would have wished.' He'd stared at his sketch and smiled ruefully. 'But I'm not too sure what she's making of my attempts so far.'

'She'll see them for what they are – an expression of your love,' she'd said gently. 'I'm so glad you decided to make the trip, Mr Rayburn.'

He nodded. 'So am I, Jennifer. I feel that this will bring closure to the sadness of recent months. But not to the happy memories – I shall always have those.'

Closure. George was not the only person on the course who was looking for closure, she thought, moving away. Hopefully, their time in Italy would achieve what both she and George wanted it to – no, what they both *needed* it to.

She'd started to look for Clare, but had suddenly realised that it was time for lunch.

She finished her coffee and stood up. They had had long enough to settle back into their work. She'd start with Clare, and that would probably be the quickest way of also finding Stephen and Nick.

Poor Clare. On the one hand, it was flattering to have two men interested in her; on the other, it could become quite tiresome, and this was pretty much what Clare had told her that morning. But the more she got to know Clare, the more confident she was that she would sort things out without causing too much pain for anyone.

She started to cross the terrace and make her way to the spot where she thought she'd find Clare. Yes, she'd do the trio next, and she'd save Max till last.

'So why did you decide to come on this course, Clare?' Jenny heard Max say as she rounded the corner of the house.

So much for leaving Max till last, she thought as she caught sight of his broad shoulders in front of her. He was sitting on his painting stool, his back to her, and looked as if he was studying his work. Clare was a little way along, parallel to him.

Jenny paused, and then moved into the shadow of a mulberry tree. Standing still, she watched him.

He changed his position, looking at his work from a different angle. A hint of muscle rippled beneath his thin shirt. His tanned forearms gleamed in the light of the sun, and with every movement of his head, streaks of gold played in his hair. She caught her breath – he really was something – and she found herself smiling with pleasure at the sight of him.

'Are you asking me that because you can see how pathetic my work is?' Clare asked him, giggling.

Jenny pulled herself sharply together. She stepped further into the shade and glanced across at Clare.

'Not at all, and I'm sure they're not.' There was laughter in Max's voice as he got up and went over to Clare. Standing behind her, he looked first at the view she was painting, then back again at her picture.

'On the other hand ...' They both laughed, and Max returned to his stool.

'My turn now.' Clare stood up and went across to have a look at his picture. 'Mmm. I see what you mean,' she said with mock gravity. 'It certainly helps to be able to see the view you're painting for real.' Smiling broadly, she returned to her work, sat down again and stared at her drawing. 'You're right,' she said with a loud sigh. 'It's rubbish. Even I can see that.'

'Jenny can say what she likes about everyone being able to learn, but I've yet to be convinced.' Max sounded amused, not critical of her, she noted with relief. Her cue to move forward.

'Did I hear someone say Jenny?' she asked, going up to them.

Max looked round at her. A warm glow stole through her at the unmistakable pleasure in his eyes.

'You did, indeed,' he said with a lazy grin. 'I was

telling Clare that my feeble scratchings are proving that not everyone can be taught to paint.' He gestured to his picture. 'There's the proof. And I'll be amazed if there's any improvement between now and the end of the week.'

A bolt of excitement shot through her.

'Are you coming to all of the classes, then?' she asked, keeping her voice as steady as she could. Extra time like this would be an unexpected bonus.

He sighed theatrically. 'I doubt if I'll be allowed to. I fully expect to be flunked as soon as you see today's offering.'

They both laughed.

'You should see my pathetic attempts, too, Jenny,' Clare called to her. 'I wish I could draw like you, but it's just not gonna happen.'

Jenny moved across to Clare and looked down at her work.

'I know you won't believe me, Clare,' she said after a moment or two, 'but your work shows promise, and I'm confident you'll see a marked improvement by the end of the week.'

'I hope you're right,' Clare said dubiously.

'You were telling me why you came on the course, Clare?' Max said, swivelling around. 'I know I shouldn't be distracting you from your masterpiece, and certainly not when Jenny's looking at it, but I'm really curious as to why you – and all the others, too – have chosen to come here. Don't mistake me – I'm glad you did – but why?'

'A moment of madness in my case, I guess. I'm training to be a nurse, and the government gives us a bursary every year. It's not a lot of money, but it means I'm not totally broke. My mates decided to go to Corfu, but can you see me on a beach all day with this hair?' She pointed to her red curls.

'Not very easily, I must admit.'

'And anyway, a beach holiday would be dead boring, so I decided to do something totally different. I didn't want to do anything practical as I do practical things all day long, and when I saw your ad, I thought to myself, that's it, I'll do something creative. It'll be fun.'

'And *are* you finding it fun?' Jenny asked.

'Actually, I am. I'm really enjoying it.'

Jenny laughed. 'I guess that was a silly question – you'd say that anyway. But I hope you mean it.' She paused. 'If you could change one thing about the week, what would you change?'

Clare thought for a moment. 'I'd have only one cool guy on the course, not two.'

Jenny gave her a rueful smile.

'I did rather notice that my nephew's smitten,' Max cut in. 'And, indeed, so is Mr Williams. But since I'm sort of an interested party, and a man, I'm above prying so I won't ask which one you prefer.'

Clare blushed. 'They both seem very nice in different ways.'

'That's a very good answer to the question I didn't ask.'

All three laughed.

'Well, as you both seem OK, I won't interrupt you any further,' Jenny said, starting to move away. 'I'll see if I can find Stephen or Nick.'

'Oh, there you are, Uncle Max. How are you getting on?' Stephen's voice came from behind her.

'I was just about to look for you, Stephen,' Jenny said, turning to him with a smile.

'I thought I'd come and see how my uncle was doing. Perhaps give him a few tips.' He sauntered over to Max's easel and leaned over him to study his work. He glanced up at the wisteria on the corner of the house, and then stared back at the picture. 'Missing that first lesson must be to blame,' he said.

Laughing, he went over to Clare. 'That's really good, Clare,' he said, his voice full of admiration. 'With *your* work, I don't even have to look at the view to know what you're painting.'

He glanced across at Max and they grinned at each other.

'You two,' Jenny said with a smile of amusement.

'I can't tell you how much I'm looking forward to scrutinising your paintings this evening, Stephen,' Max said cheerfully. 'I'm sure I'll have much to learn from them.'

'I'm not sure I should let you see what I've done: the quality of my work might make you give up on the spot.'

'Ah, but you've no choice in the matter. If you look at today's programme, you'll see that our work's going to be on display before dinner. What's more, we're going to have more than one occasion on which to gaze in awe at what we've all done in the day.'

'Mmm,' Stephen said, a mock-serious expression on his face. 'I think you should skip that part of the programme, old man. Any sudden strain could damage your health, and I dread to think what might happen if you heard honest comments about your work.'

'Your concern is deeply touching, but my aged bones and I will risk it. After all, we have a nurse among us.'

'So we do.' Stephen turned and beamed at Clare. 'But if anyone's going to need Clare to resuscitate them, I want it to be me.'

Clare blushed.

'What did you paint this afternoon, Stephen?' Jenny asked, changing the subject. 'In fact, why don't we leave Max and Clare in peace and you can show me what you've been doing?'

Footsteps sounded on the gravel path, and they turned their heads as Nick came into sight.

'So that's where you've all got to,' he exclaimed. 'I might have guessed.'

'I'm afraid Jenny's rather got caught up here, paralysed by the brilliance of our work,' Max told Nick with a grin.

'Huh.' Stephen sniggered.

'Come on, you two,' Jenny said, moving across to

Stephen and Nick. 'I'd like you to show me what you've done.'

As she walked past Max, she couldn't resist glancing down at him. To her surprise, he was staring up at her. Their eyes met, and held. Her steps slowed, and stopped.

For a long moment, the world hung in suspense and she saw only Max.

Then abruptly she jerked her head away.

Hurrying after Nick and Stephen, she struggled to summon the image of her father to her mind.

'That was a colossal meal,' Howard said, rubbing his stomach. 'I'm not sure I'll be able to get up from the table.'

Jenny laughed. 'Maria had something similar in mind for lunch, too. Can you imagine eating two such huge meals in one day?' she asked, addressing the table as a whole. 'How Italians manage to stay as slim as they do, I don't know. Not all of them, of course, but the majority.'

Clare sighed enviously. 'They must have magic ways of burning off the calories. I just wish they'd share them with us Brits.'

'You're gorgeous as you are, Clare,' Nick said. He put his arm round the back of her chair. She moved forward and he dropped his arm.

Paula smiled vaguely in Jenny's direction, and then turned to Max, who was next to her. 'Howie and I were saying earlier how flattered we were that you were choosing to spend so much of your precious time with little old us.' She tinkled a silvery laugh, took an *amoretto* from the bowl in the centre of the table and popped it into her mouth.

Jenny groaned inwardly. Paula and Howard could easily bore Max into staying away, she thought in a moment of despair. Their silly twitterings were hardly the adult conversation he'd sought. She couldn't let them monopolise him, but what on earth could she do to stop them?

At that moment, Max glanced at her across the table and smiled. She felt herself relax a little, smiled back, and then forced herself to turn to George, who was sitting next to her.

'I think there's definitely been some progress in your use of the brush, Mr Rayburn,' she said, trying hard at the same time to listen to Howard and Paula's conversation with Max.

'All I can say is,' Max was telling Paula, 'I'm enjoying myself enormously. I'm very grateful to all of you for letting me join in. Originally, I'd only intended to come over in the evenings, but I seem to have become a fixture in the day, too. It's certainly a very different week from the one I'd've had if you hadn't been here – but it's turning into a very interesting one.'

'What would you have been doing if we hadn't been here? You don't seem to be the sort of person who'd lie by a pool all day long and do nothing,' Howard said, sliding his arm around the back of Paula's chair and leaning a little closer to Max.

'I'd have a swim before breakfast, and again in the afternoon, but I suppose I do that now, anyway. But you're right, lying in the sun isn't for me. If you weren't here, I'd probably spend more time relaxing on the *loggia* – the veranda that runs around part of the house.'

'It sounds heavenly,' Paula sighed.

'It is. I expect that I'd linger there, reading or looking at the view. Being on a slope means that there's usually a gentle breeze so it's all very pleasant. But having said that,' he added with a laugh, 'knowing me, the truth is I'd probably go back to my computer and work out of habit. I suspect that I'm going to have more of a rest by joining the class than I would've done by staying on my own.'

'Your life here sounds idyllic,' Paula sighed, 'computer or not. Don't you think so, Howie?'

'Absolutely. I'm like you about work, Max. If I was holidaying here, I'd need a hobby to keep my mind off my job. Books are only OK for so long.' He slipped his arm from the back of Paula's chair to her shoulder. 'Nope, I'd have to do something other than just read and swim.'

'I couldn't sit still and read all day any more than you could,' Max agreed. 'But I'm extremely lucky that I can pursue my interests in both England and Umbria: I've been collecting pictures in a small way over the years. It's just a hobby, but I love it, and I've every intention of spending a large part of my time in Italy visiting galleries and exploring little shops in out-of-the-way places. Who knows, I might find a hitherto-undiscovered masterpiece,' he added with a laugh.

'Ooh, what fun,' Paula declared. 'Isn't it, Howie?'

'It certainly is. I envy you, Max.'

'And galleries and museums aren't the only places to visit. Nearly every church, no matter how small the town, has at least one painting worth seeing. In fact, I'd planned to take Stephen round some of the nearby churches this week. Funnily enough, though, just after I told him of my plan, he confessed to a burning desire to join the art class.'

Out of the corner of her eye, Jenny saw him glance affectionately at Stephen, who was deep in conversation with Nick and Clare. Then she felt Max's eyes come to rest on her. Struggling not to look at him, she tossed her blonde plait over her shoulder, kept her face firmly turned towards George, and made a great effort to focus on what he was saying.

'Jenny seems very easy to get along with, and a good teacher, too,' she heard Max say as he turned back to Howard and Paula.

So he thought she was easy to get along with, did he? A glow of happiness crept through her body.

'Oh, she is. She's a lovely person. Howie and I have already learnt so much from her. But about your hobby, Max. You're lucky to have the luxury of buying paintings – most people can't afford much more than food and drink. It's—'

'Paula,' Howard said sharply. He sounded distinctly annoyed, Jenny thought. She glanced at him in surprise and saw him frowning.

Paula's laugh was shrill. 'I was only going to say that I'm so pleased that someone's able to preserve all these wonderful paintings, Max.'

Howard nodded. 'She's right about that.'

'But we look like having a fine collection of our own to take home with us, don't we, Howie?' Paula added. 'Jenny said some very kind things about our work.'

'I hope you do,' Max said with a smile. 'It'd make the week worthwhile for you, and it'd make Jenny very happy, I'm sure.'

His eyes returned to Jenny's face.

'Are your paintings here or in England?' Howard asked.

Max pulled his gaze away. 'Mostly in England. I've got a few pictures here as well, but my main collection is at home. But don't get carried away and imagine rooms full of Leonardos. It's only a very modest collection, something I do for fun.'

Howard picked up the bottle of dessert wine, leaned in front of Paula and divided the last of the wine between his glass and Max's. 'What style of art do you go for?'

'I'd say I was quite eclectic – a bit of everything, but contemporary art probably predominates. Certainly, the pictures I've got on my walls here are contemporary. And the ones in this house, too.'

'Did you bring them over from England?' Howard asked.

'That's right. I know that these are fourteenth-century houses, but I felt that contemporary art would go better with the style of furniture I've chosen. Classical wouldn't work as well.'

'I love looking at paintings.' Paula's voice was tinged with wistfulness.

'From what I saw this evening, you're a pretty good artist yourself, Paula. Your work today was really impressive.'

'You're just saying that, Max,' she simpered.

'Not at all. Out of all of us, you and Howard are the only ones who seem to have a natural flair. Any flair, at all, for that matter. I reckon you could be extremely good if you wanted to. I'm sure you'd be able to sell your work.'

'It's sweet of you to say that, Max, but I'm sure I wouldn't. Who'd want to buy anything painted by little old me?' She giggled.

'Paula was told the same thing at school,' Howard said, glancing affectionately at his wife, his irritation clearly gone. 'But it's a difficult business to succeed in and she's never attempted to make it her career. It's always been a bit of a regret, which is one of the reasons why we chose this sort of week for our honeymoon. It's a moment of luxury amid the humdrum of everyday life.'

'I wondered why you'd come here and not gone somewhere like the Maldives,' Max remarked.

'Ugh.' Howard grimaced. 'The very thought of it. As I said before, we'd be bored stiff, doing nothing but sitting in the sun by a hotel pool. We've got the sun here, and a pool, but we've got something more, too. No, this is ideal for us.'

Max smiled broadly at them. 'I'm glad that it's living up to expectations.'

'Oh, it is,' Paula said tremulously. She paused a moment, and ran her finger round the rim of her water glass. 'Can I be very naughty?' she asked in a little girl voice. Pouting, she glanced at Howard, and then back at Max. 'Howie's going to be very angry with me – he said I mustn't ask you.' She stopped and bit her lip.

'Ask me what?' Max prompted.

'If we could take a little peek at your paintings. We've seen the ones here, so we guessed you must have others in your house, and we'd love to see them.' Her words came out in a rush.

How rude, Jenny thought in annoyance. She glanced at Max's face, wondering how he'd handle it. They'd gone too far and she wondered if he'd drop the genial exterior and say so.

Howard took his arm from Paula's shoulder, looked reprovingly at her, and then glanced apologetically at Max. 'I'm really sorry, Max. Paula shouldn't have asked you that – your house is private.' He turned back to Paula. 'You know Max's house is off limits. Nick told us Jenny said that when Stephen offered the use of Max's internet.'

Paula gave an embarrassed laugh. 'Silly me. I forgot. Please, don't be angry with me, Howie. I'm sorry Max. I seem to be saying all the wrong things this evening.'

'You don't need to see Max's paintings,' Howard went on, as if she hadn't spoken. 'There are paintings everywhere you turn in Italy. And as for the internet, we can always use the café in Montefalco when it's open.' He turned to Max. 'Paula knows that perfectly well.'

'How remiss of me,' Max exclaimed in annoyance. 'I never got round to sorting out your internet. I meant to have a landline and Wi-Fi installed in this house, too, but in the rush of being ready to open on time, it got overlooked. Of course, you can use my computer. Just ask me whenever you want to come across. And by all means have a look at my pictures at the same time. It's the least I can do – I'm invading your space every night, after all.' He smiled at them both.

Still the even-tempered man, Jenny thought, frowning slightly. No sign of a different sort of man beneath the surface – a man who could drive her father to his death. She really didn't know what to think. He seemed so different from the man she'd heard about over the years.

Paula and Howard glanced at each other. 'That's very sporting of you, Max; thank you,' Howard said. 'I still feel badly that Paula asked you, though.'

'Yes, thank you so much, Max.' She turned to Howard. 'Oh, Howie darling! I'm the happiest bride alive.'

Jenny glanced from Paula, whose face was wreathed in smiles, to Max. His expression was inscrutable. She looked down at her plate, and bit her lip in sudden anxiety and confusion.

Chapter Seven

Jenny turned round at the sound of footsteps approaching the table.

'Max,' she exclaimed, and felt a momentary embarrassment at how pleased she'd sounded at seeing him there. 'I didn't expect to see you again until dinner. I thought we'd worn you out this morning and you were going to have a break from us this afternoon.'

'I thought so, too,' he said, sitting down opposite her, 'which is why I disappeared at the end of the class. But you get used to having company, and it suddenly felt quite lonely, sitting on my own with my coffee, knowing that you were so close – that all of you were close by – so I decided on the spur of the moment to hitch a lift with you into Bevagna.' He paused. 'I hope you don't mind,' he added, a trace of awkwardness in his voice.

A wave of pleasure surged through her at the thought of spending the whole afternoon with him. The degree of pleasure she felt took her quite by surprise. But of course, having more time with him brought her goal that much nearer. No wonder she was delighted.

'Not at all,' she said, beaming at him. 'And I know the others won't mind either. They were saying at lunch how much they were looking forward to seeing you this evening.'

'Which reminds me, Jenny. I didn't get a chance to ask you this morning, but you looked a bit worried last night. Is everything all right?'

'Everything's perfect,' she said quickly. 'It's just that Paula seemed to be going a bit over the top – I couldn't help overhearing – and I was worried you might be bored. I wouldn't want you to stop coming across to us. That's to say, none of us would ...'

'You needn't worry on that score. It would take a lot

more than Paula to put me off joining you in the day, or at dinner for that matter. I'm enjoying myself far much too much.'

Relief swept through her, and she felt her tension drain away. Until that moment, she hadn't realised the strain she'd been under since the evening before, when she'd had to listen to Paula and Howard hassle Max and been unable to do anything about it.

'I'm glad to hear it. You coming to Bevagna is a bonus for us. You'll be able to add to what I've already told the group about the town – you must know it so much better than I do. I read up about it before I came, but I only had time to go there twice in the week before everyone arrived, and that was mainly to work out how to organise today's visit.'

'You won't need any help from me, I'm sure. Your handouts this morning covered everything imaginable. I was quite impressed.'

She laughed. 'I'll take that as a compliment. From the short amount of time I've spent with you, I'd say that you're not easily impressed.'

'You make me sound quite formidable,' he remarked with a grin. 'Like a bad guy from a Dickensian novel, or a domineering sort of father who demands impossibly high standards from his children.'

'Dickensian?' She slowly ran her eyes down his face, lingering a moment on his lips. 'I don't think so,' she said lightly. Her look returned to the dark eyes that were gazing at her with open warmth. 'And certainly not like a domineering father.'

There was an imperceptible pause on his part. 'Good. I wouldn't want to come across as unreachable. I wouldn't like that at all, Jenny,' he added quietly.

Their eyes met across the table, and neither moved for a long moment.

'It's time I got my things ready for this afternoon,' she said, and she stood up.

* * *

63

They stepped off the minibus, crossed a small patch of grass and stared ahead of them at the ancient pink and grey stone bridge which spanned the river flowing around the walled town of Bevagna. Beneath the arch, clear green water reflected the pillared colonnade of the building on the other side.

'Wow,' Stephen said. 'That's some view.'

'The building reflected in the water is the old wash house,' Jenny told them. 'When we cross the bridge, you'll be able to see where the women used to scrub their clothes. There's a weir there, too. The view from this spot is one of my favourite of the town. I think it's beautiful.'

'And what a lovely drive that was, Jennifer,' George said, shaking the stiffness out of his knee. 'I'm quite astounded by the number of wineries in the short distance we've travelled.'

'I know. It's amazing, isn't it, not just the number of wineries but the quality of the wine in the area?' She looked around at the group. 'Well, welcome to Bevagna. Like most Umbrian towns, Bevagna's a small Roman town, which also has some medieval remains. Unlike most of the other towns, though, it's not on a hilltop. Apart from one or two slight dips, it's all on one level.'

'Thank you, dear lady,' George murmured.

They all laughed.

She pointed towards the stone wall of the car park. 'We're going to go up those few steps now and then cross over the bridge and go through the gateway into the town. It's one of several gateways into Bevagna. Then we'll walk to the main square, Piazza Silvestri. It won't take us long as it really is a very small town. It can't be more than two hundred metres in diameter.'

'That is small,' Howard exclaimed.

'But there are still lots of things to see, as you know. Several of the most interesting places are in the Piazza Silvestri itself, so you won't have to go far. Now, you've each got the town plan I gave you—'

'Oh, dear, I forgot mine,' Nick cut in. 'I'll have to share yours, Clare.'

Jenny noticed Stephen turn sharply and glare at Nick. Disappointment clouded Clare's face, and she glanced surreptitiously at Stephen, who gave her a rueful smile. So that's the way the land lies, is it, she thought. Good.

'I'll point out one or two places on the way,' she continued, 'but for most of the afternoon, it'll be up to you what you see or don't see, and what you draw. Don't forget to allow plenty of time for your picture. As soon as we reach the *piazza*, we'll get our bearings, fix a time to regroup and then split up. I'll give you time to look around, decide what to draw and make a start on it. And after a while, I'll wander around and see how you're getting on.'

'Why don't you give yourself a break and leave that agony till this evening?' Nick suggested with a grin. 'Why ruin your afternoon?'

She smiled. 'I'll risk it, Nick, but thanks for your consideration. If you don't forget what we said about composition and colour this morning, I think you'll all be pleasantly surprised by what you achieve and I'll be in for a treat this evening. We all will.'

'We'll do our best, won't we, Howie?' Paula gave a little laugh and looked round at the others.

'Right, if you're ready,' Jenny said, 'we can set off.'

'What about our easels and things?' Clare asked as they started to move.

'Carlo's bringing them to the *piazza* for us.' They turned in unison and looked at Carlo, who was in the middle of taking a small pull-cart from the back of the minibus. 'Come on, then, off we go,' she said, and she turned to lead the way up the steps to the bridge.

As she started to walk across, followed by the group, she saw Paula grab Howard's hand and start to pull him towards Max. Damn, she thought.

But Max moved more quickly than Paula, and a moment

later, he was walking at Jenny's side, a short distance ahead of the group.

'That was a close thing,' he muttered, wiping his forehead in mock relief.

She laughed. 'So you saw what Paula was up to, did you? So did I. I'm beginning to think that the Andersons are the sort of people who like to be friends with the boss, so to speak. They certainly seem to be obsessed with you,' she added as they reached the other side of the bridge.

'I reckon you're right. Every time I turn round, I'm in danger of tripping over one of them or both.'

'And that still didn't put you off coming this afternoon?'

'Not at all. I felt like having some company and I love the town. Compact though it is, you come across something new on every visit. But I must confess, I do have an ulterior motive, one that I didn't tell you about earlier.'

'You do?' Suddenly nervous about what he was going to say, she drew in a deep breath, and held it.

He nodded. 'I've ordered a fruit bowl from a man who has a shop here. He sculptures glass and his work is outstanding. I wanted a particular shade of sea green and I knew the exact shape it should be. He said he'd make it for me, and apparently it's ready now. I thought I could collect it today and have a look round his showroom at the same time. It's only small.'

She released her breath, and smiled at him. 'That's a lot of thought to put into a fruit bowl. I hope the finished product lives up to your expectations.'

'Why don't you come with me and see if it does? After all, getting to know you better was another reason for coming today,' he added lightly.

She opened her mouth to say that she'd better not go with him, but nothing came out.

'And don't say that you've got to stay near the others,' he cut in quickly. 'As you said, it's a tiny town. You couldn't be far from them at any time even if you wanted to, and it'll be ages before they do any painting. We could go to the glass shop and then have a drink in one of the piazzas. I often go to a place in Piazza Garibaldi and sit on the terrace there. I'd enjoy talking to you about some of the things you've seen while you've been here. I seldom get the chance to discuss anything artistic with someone who knows what they're talking about.'

'What about the people you buy your pictures from?'

'That's different: they're professionals. I was talking about ordinary people.'

'Flatter me, why don't you?' she laughed.

He grinned at her. 'You know what I mean. And then after our drink, you can go off and survey the endeavours of all while I have a crack at doing a picture myself. I'm going to draw one of the gargoyles over the main doorway of the Church of San Michele Arcangelo. They're quite striking. So, how about the fruit bowl followed by a drink?'

'It sounds fun. Thank you, I'd love to come along with you.'

'Great.' She heard genuine pleasure in his voice and she turned towards him at the same moment as he glanced at her. Their steps slowed, and they stopped in the large open space on the other side of the bridge, facing each other.

She felt a sudden overwhelming desire to touch his face, to run her hand lightly down his cheek, to feel his skin beneath her fingertips. She wanted to look away – knew she must look away – but she was powerless to do so. She couldn't stop herself: her eyes slowly traced his laughter lines, his nose, the slight cleft in his chin. A lock of hair fell over his forehead. He raised his hand to push it back, and she breathed in the citrus tang of fresh shampoo. Her gaze returned to his mouth, and her lips fell slightly apart.

'Jenny,' he said, his voice so low that she wasn't even sure that she'd heard him right.

Dragging her eyes from his face, she forced herself to turn back to the path ahead and start walking again, moving swiftly to get ahead of him.

She must stop herself from thinking about him that

way, she thought in a panic, her heart pounding fast. If she didn't, she'd send out the wrong signals. And they *would be* the wrong signals – they had to be.

Being friends with him was part of the plan, but no more than friends. And not real friends at that. This was all a charade, a way of getting him to open up. It couldn't ever be anything else – not with one of the men responsible for her father's death. Whatever her body was telling her, it was something that couldn't be. Not with him.

She felt like bursting into tears.

She walked faster and saw the *piazza* ahead of her.

'We're almost there now,' she called back to him, her voice strange to her ears.

He caught up with her. She glanced quickly at him, and saw confusion in his eyes.

'I'm sorry I ran off,' she said with an awkward smile. 'I want to try and get us a spot by the fountain. It can get quite busy,' she added lamely.

'If you think so,' he said. He sounded unsure.

'I do. It's only sensible.' They both fell silent.

'I've a pretty good idea what George will choose to draw,' Max said after a few moments. 'In fact, I'd put money on it.' His voice took on a note of amusement.

She smiled at him, hugely relieved that they seemed to have returned to their normal banter. 'What do you think he'll do, then?'

'The frieze above the door of the Church of San Silvestro. There's a small mountain which has got four streams on it and a growing vine. I bet he focuses on the vine. It's meant to represent the Church or God, but I doubt that our George will be thinking about its symbolic interpretation.'

She giggled. 'I don't think I should be listening to this.'

'Don't get me wrong, he's a really nice man, and I very much enjoyed talking to him at coffee this morning. But I'm not sure that his heightened colour can be put down to spiritual fervour, despite the fact that we're surrounded by churches and museums replete with religious paintings.'

Laughing, she glanced back at the group. Seeing that the others were dawdling and were still some way behind them, she stopped walking. 'We'd better wait a moment. We're almost there and I haven't pointed out a single thing so far.'

'Come on; they'll be fine. After all, they've got a map. We'll wait for them when we get to the square. To be honest, I'm enjoying being able to talk to you without anyone interrupting us.'

It was a sentiment they shared, she thought. But for different reasons. She felt a wave of regret start to wash over her again, and she swallowed hard. She must keep her focus on how to profit from her time alone with him, and not on how much she was enjoying talking to him and being with him. Yes, he was great company and he clearly had a good sense of humour – the sexiest characteristic a man could have, she'd always thought – but having fun wasn't the reason she was there.

Originally, she'd thought that him coming across in the evenings would give her enough time to get to know him. But it hadn't worked out like that. The others all wanted to speak to him, too, and he obliged them all. In fact, she spoke to him less than to anyone else at dinner. But the week was flying by at a frightening speed. This afternoon in Bevagna was the best quality time she'd had with him so far, and she couldn't afford to waste a precious second of it.

'Fortunately, your fears of a large crowd around the fountain haven't materialised,' Max remarked, breaking into her thoughts as they reached the Piazza Silvestri and went across to the fountain to wait for the others.

'Fortunately, you're right,' she said, looking around.

After a moment or two of silence, he glanced down at her. 'Perhaps I shouldn't have told you that I was enjoying talking to you. It seems to have been a real conversation killer. You've been miles away ever since I said that.'

She gave an awkward laugh. 'Oh, I'm sorry. I've been

mentally rehearsing what to say to the class before I send them off to have a look around. I thought I ought to remind them what there is to see.'

'As I said before, they've got a map. Ah, here they are. And no surprises who's first.'

'What a pretty little town this is,' Paula enthused as she and Howard came up to them. 'It's so very sweet. We just couldn't help stopping and looking at everything.'

Clare, Stephen and Nick followed close behind them, with George only a short distance away.

When he'd reached them, they all gathered around Jenny.

'Before we go our separate ways,' she said, 'there are just a couple of things to tell you. Carlo will be staying in front of the bar over there. He'll have your painting equipment with him.' She pointed to a small bar on the corner of the square, outside of which a few men were sitting on colourful upright chairs. 'When you've seen all you want to see and are ready to start drawing, come and collect your things from him.'

They nodded.

'If you're thirsty, you can pick up something from the bar here or from the one in Piazza Garibaldi, which is near the remains of the Roman temple. There are several little shops, which sell specialities of the region, but they won't be open till later. I don't know if you still want to do any shopping, Paula, but you're probably better hanging on until Assisi tomorrow, if you can.' She turned and pointed to the fountain. 'As you can see, the fountain has a couple of water spouts. If you want, you can drink from them, although personally I never drink from a fountain, whatever the sign says.'

Max nodded. 'I'm with Jenny on that. I'd follow her advice, if I were you.' The warmth in his voice embraced her.

Suddenly self-conscious, she raised her hand and smoothed down her hair.

'Where was I?' she said, trying to get her thoughts back on track. 'Oh, yes, talking about water. Do try and see the old Roman baths. They're under a building that's accessed through a side door. It's marked on the map. You have to ring the bell at number two, which is the house on the left, and ask the custodian to let you in, but it's free of charge.'

'Think I'll give that a miss. I've seen Roman baths before,' Nick said.

'That may be,' Max cut in, 'but this is the most magnificent sheet of mosaic flooring that I've seen anywhere. The details on the sea creatures are quite amazing. A display on one of the walls shows you what the bath would have looked like two thousand years ago and how the Romans would have used it. Believe me, it's worth a visit.'

'Howie and I are definitely going to go there before we go anywhere else,' Paula said quickly. 'Aren't we, Howie?'

'Whatever makes you happy, sweetheart.'

Jenny smiled around at the group. 'Is there anything anyone wants to ask me?'

They shook their heads.

'It's three o'clock now. Why don't we meet here again at six-thirty? That will give you plenty of time to see all you want, and the shops will have been open for a little while in case you want to have a quick browse through them before we leave. Hopefully, you'll have managed to fit a drawing in, too. I'll try to get round to all of you at some point during the afternoon. Well, I see that Carlo's in position now, so off you go.'

'And a most attractive position it is, too,' she heard George remark to Nick, indicating Carlo, who had joined the men sitting in front of the bar.

She turned to Max. The others had gone, and they were completely alone at last. Despite the daunting task ahead of her, she couldn't help feeling a frisson of excitement.

Chapter Eight

Jenny leaned forward and helped herself to a small tomato *bruschetta*.

'I really shouldn't be eating this,' she said, popping it into her mouth. 'I had a very good lunch, and I know what Maria's got planned for this evening. I'll be enormous by the time I'm back in England.'

'I don't think you've anything to worry about,' Max said warmly. Their eyes met across the table but both immediately looked away. He glanced round the almost-empty square. 'I had the right idea, bringing you here,' he said. 'It's never as crowded as it is in Silvestri. Paula and Howard will be long gone by now – we were in the shop for quite a while – and if any of the other budding Picassos had thought about venturing all the way across the town, you mentioning a Roman temple in the vicinity is bound to have put them off. I'm sure we're safe for a bit.'

She laughed. 'I think you're being a little hard on them.'

He grinned. 'Maybe.'

'But I will admit that not one of them, not even Paula, comes close to having the same degree of interest in art and aesthetics as you do, Max. And I'm not just talking about your collection of paintings and the galleries you visit. Look at the care you're taking over the interior of your house, and it isn't even your main home. How many other people would bother about the colour and shape of a fruit bowl?'

'I suppose you're right. I hadn't really thought about it, but the family business is textiles, and that requires an eye for colour, texture and design. I guess those interests are in my genes.' He leaned forward to take a truffle-topped *bruschetta*.

At the same moment Jenny reached for another tomato one. Their hands touched. Sparks of electricity winged up her bare arm, and she pulled quickly back.

'Go on,' he said, pushing the plate towards her. 'Have another one. If you don't, I'll feel guilty about eating so many.'

'Oh, all right, then.' Her skin still tingling, she reached for the *bruschetta*. She bit into it, and stopped – he'd just mentioned his family and she'd almost missed it! It may have only been a passing remark, but this was the opening she'd been waiting for, and she should've instantly seen it. What on earth was the matter with her? She must pull herself together, and fast.

She swallowed the mouthful of *bruschetta*. 'Are your parents as interested in interior decoration as you are, Max?' she asked, keeping her voice casual.

'I've never really thought about it. They certainly took great care over the pictures they hung on their walls. They didn't have a collection as such, though. And not one of us – not me, not my parents, not my brother – was any good at drawing. We're not creative in that way: just appreciative.'

He'd mentioned Peter, and she couldn't not build on this.

She felt cold all over. She was going to have to remind him that he'd lost his brother. She hated the idea of doing such a horrible thing, but he might think it strange if she didn't pick up on the mention of him. And this could be the only chance she'd have to talk about his family. No, she'd no choice but to make the most of it.

She made a conscious effort to think of her mother's features, etched with a grief that had lasted so many years, and she took a deep breath.

'When I first saw your advert, I googled your company and I couldn't help seeing the obituaries for your brother. I'm so sorry, Max. He was very young to die. And Stephen was very young to lose his father. It must have been terrible for your family.'

'It was,' he said quietly. 'Really terrible. I'd never want to live through a time like that again. Peter was eight years older than me, but despite our age difference he was my best friend. I joined the family business very young – I used to help in the office when I was still at school, and I joined the company full-time when I was sixteen. Peter was there for me every step of the way. That probably made us even closer. Stephen was only fourteen when his dad died. I've tried to be a stand-in father to him, but I know he still misses Peter. And so do I.'

'I'm so sorry, perhaps you'd rather not talk about him.'

'No, it's OK. He'll always be a very important part of my life and I wouldn't want him to be forgotten, or to be someone who could only be mentioned in hushed tones. I'm not saying he was an angel, mind you – he wasn't. He made decisions I didn't agree with and I told him so, but he was a terrific brother and I'm happy to have a chance to talk about him. Anyway, that's enough about me. What about you? Are your parents artists?'

'I don't know about my dad, but my mother could have been very good. Unfortunately, though, she could only paint as a hobby.' She paused, and then quickly went on. 'She was very young when she had me, and she and my father had a lot of financial worries so there just wasn't enough time and money for her to take it seriously.'

'What does your father do?'

For a moment she wondered whether she should end the deception that was beginning to tear her apart, and tell him the truth. But the moment passed: it was just too soon in their friendship. 'He had his own business. Stephen and I have something in common – my father also died when I was young. Afterwards, my mother lost any desire to paint. She hasn't picked up a brush since then, and I don't think she ever will again.'

'I'm sorry for asking you something that led to a sad memory.' He paused for a moment. 'But they would have come up at some point – your father and Peter, I mean.'

A chill ran through her. Had he guessed who she was?

'Why do you say that?' Her voice seemed to come from far away.

He stared into her face. 'Because I want to get to know you better,' he said quietly. 'Until today, I've only been scratching the surface. I may not have known you for long, Jenny, but it's been long enough for me to know that I want to learn much more about you.'

She relaxed again. 'How funny,' she said, her voice shaking a little. 'I feel exactly the same about you.' She felt herself start to blush.

'Well, if we're going to delve deep below the surface, perhaps we should anaesthetise ourselves first. How about another white wine? We've got the time.'

'I'll have an Aperol soda this time, please. I've still got to have a look at everyone's work, and I don't want to be seeing double when I do my rounds.'

He laughed and stood up. 'You're right about that. I'm sure that one of each noble effort will be more than enough. I'll be back in a minute.' He disappeared into the dark interior of the restaurant.

Jenny stared around the *piazza*, biting her lip. They'd finally got on to the subject of their families, which was a huge leap forward, and he'd even gone as far as to hint about things that his company had got wrong in the past. Perhaps he'd even been thinking about her father. She'd love to know, but she couldn't ask him yet. No, she couldn't have asked for the afternoon to have gone better. So why did she feel so flat, she wondered.

Max returned to the table, closely followed by a waiter who was carrying a tray of drinks.

He sat down. 'I've asked for some more of the *crostini* with wild boar *pâté*,' he said as the waiter put their drinks in front of them. 'I'm having the same as you: it looks refreshing.'

'Did you make yourself understood in there?' she asked with a smile.

He laughed. 'We'll soon find out. I certainly hope so. I know that *cinghiale* is wild boar, but if they didn't understand *pâté*, we could have a problem of enormous dimensions on a tiny bit of toasted bread. Cheers.' He raised his glass to her.

'*Salute*,' she reciprocated, and took a sip of her drink. 'Are you planning on spending a lot of time in Italy, Max? After all, you seem to be treating your house as more than just a holiday home, putting good paintings on the walls and paying a lot of attention to items like fruit bowls.'

'I hope to come over several times a year, even if I can only stay for a few days at a time on some of the visits. I intend to stay for the whole of every August, though, and I see the art courses as being one of the highlights of the summer.'

'Even with people like Paula on them? She should never have asked to see your paintings or use the internet. She knows your house is off-limits – I told them so at the start of the week.'

'It's not a problem. I should've arranged for the internet to be installed before they got here – not everyone has a smartphone and it's reasonable for them to want to check their e-mails. I'll sort that out before next year.'

'That's very kind of you, but if you change your mind, I can easily have a word with Howard and Paula.'

'It's nothing. I really don't mind.' He leaned closer to her. 'But what's far from nothing is the fact that I promised to take you to a local restaurant to sample their *tagliatelle al tartufo*. As you can see, I haven't forgotten.'

She laughed. 'Don't worry – you were just being polite. I won't hold you to your promise. After all, we were just joking around, weren't we?'

'Isn't there a saying, many a true promise is spoken in jest?'

She laughed again. 'If you say so.'

'I do. A promise is a promise and we shall go.' She opened her mouth to speak, but he held up his hand. 'Stop. I know what you're going to say. We'll go, but not while the class is here. It's pretty obvious that you can't leave them for the whole evening: you're the one who's holding the different elements together and you need to be there. I shall just have to be patient.'

'So when do you suggest we go, then?' she asked, trying to quell the sense of excitement that was welling up inside her.

'On Saturday evening. The group will be leaving for home throughout the day, but I think I'm right in saying that they'll all be gone by late afternoon. You're bound to be feeling a bit lonely when they've left, and actually, so will I. Going out to dinner together will be the perfect way to end the week.'

'What about Stephen?'

'There's enough to keep him amused at the house. If he's truly desperate, he could make a start on his university work. So, is that agreed?'

She looked up from her drink and stared at him. In the depths of his eyes, there was unmistakable admiration. But there was something else, too.

'Yes, it is,' she said, her voice strange to her ears. 'Thank you. I'm already looking forward to it.'

And she realised that despite her determination to keep her emotions in check, she really was.

Chapter Nine

Jenny stared in satisfaction at the collection of traditional and contemporary watercolours arranged around the perimeters of the terrace. She felt totally shattered, and very relieved that she'd decided to display the work of well-known watercolour artists and not the work they'd done in Assisi that day.

Showing them work done by others was going to be so much easier than critiquing each other's efforts, which was anything but relaxing for the group and downright exhausting for her. The only person who probably wouldn't be worn out that evening was Max, who'd stayed at home. The rest of them had spent most of the day walking around Assisi, and what they needed was a peaceful evening in which to recharge their batteries.

'Aha, here you are,' Nick said cheerfully, coming out on to the terrace. He stopped and stared at the paintings. 'So this is the exhibition for Wednesday, is it? The standard's slightly higher than the other nights, isn't it? Forget that. It's much higher than the last few evenings.'

Summoning up every ounce of energy that she could, she turned to Nick and gave him a broad smile. 'Hello, Nick. It's unlike you to be the first here.'

He grinned at her. 'I like to be unpredictable. It keeps 'em guessing.'

She laughed. 'I see. It's all part of your allure, is it?'

'I used to think so.' He gave her a rueful grin. 'But something tells me that my allure has faded a bit.'

'I won't pretend that I don't know what you're talking about. Cue for alcohol, I'm inclined to think. Why don't I pour us a drink and you can tell me about it? If you want to, that is.'

'You sit down; I'll do the pouring.' He went across to the side table, took a bottle of Prosecco from the bed of ice and started to open it. 'I bet Stephen would hate it if he caught me making the drinks – he seems to have adopted the role of bartender for the week.' He filled two glasses, handed one to her, and they sat down at the end of the dinner table, which had been set up under the awning. 'I guess it's pretty obvious that the bartender's job isn't the only thing that I'd like to take from him.'

'I did notice that he and Clare disappeared as soon as we got to Assisi. It's a shame for you, Nick, but I'm afraid that one of you had to lose out, if not both. After all, there was no guarantee that Clare would feel anything for either of you.'

'I know that. But to concede defeat to someone younger than I am, who's still at university – it's pathetic. Mind you, he's got a load of dosh behind him. He's not exactly a student struggling on a pittance.'

'You don't think that Clare ...'

'No. It sounded as if I do, but I don't; not at all. Clare's not like that. I'm just enjoying piling on the agony. It's the masochist in me.'

'It's a pity there isn't a second unattached female on the course,' she said sympathetically.

'You can say that again. Although, come to think of it, there is.' He grinned at her. 'There's you, Jenny.' She started in surprise. 'I know you're a year or two older than I am, but that'd suit me just fine – I've always fancied being a toyboy. And you're very pretty – all big blue eyes and blonde hair. In fact, the more I think about it, the more I think you'd be ideal for me. Just imagine it – I could have private art lessons every day.'

She laughed awkwardly. 'Slow down, Nick. I'm glad to see that your heart isn't irredeemably broken, but I'm not looking for a man at the moment. I need to find a job first, decide where to live, all that sort of thing. I'm just here to teach – I've no hidden agenda.'

But she *did* have a hidden agenda. Her guilt at having to lie to Nick prickled, and she took a hasty sip of her drink.

'But I'd fail there, too, wouldn't I?' he said, carrying on as if she hadn't spoken.

She looked up from her drink, startled. 'What do you mean by that?'

'You and Max. If you're not an item now, you soon will be. I've seen the way he looks at you when you don't know it. I bet you're the only reason he's picked up a paint brush this week.'

Her heart gave a sudden thud. 'You're completely wrong about that. He's friendly and he likes talking about art, but it's no more than that.'

'And every instinct tells me that you fancy him like mad. You're as bad as he is, always watching him when he's not aware of it.'

'Really, Nick. You've got it totally wrong; it's not like that at all.' She felt a sudden anxiety, and bit her lip.

'Maybe, but I don't think so.' He stared morosely into his glass, and sighed. 'And I definitely haven't got it wrong about Clare really liking Stephen. I wish I could hate him for it, but I can't. He's a pretty cool guy.'

'But getting a girl this week would have been no more than a bonus, wouldn't it? That wasn't the reason you came on the course – or at least, I'd be very surprised if it were. You weren't to know that you'd meet someone like Clare. If you wanted to find yourself a girlfriend, internet dating would have been a much safer bet, and probably a lot less expensive.'

He smiled at her. 'You're right. I didn't come looking for love.'

'So why *did* you decide to do the course, Nick? If you don't mind me saying so, you're not the sort of person I would have expected to choose to spend his holiday learning how to use watercolour.'

'I don't mind you saying so at all – in fact, I consider it a compliment.' He grinned at her. 'Sorry and all that, but it is. First of all, it's not my proper holiday – I'm going with my mates to Cyprus in August. This week's just an extra.

I had some holiday to use up, saw the ad for the classes, and signed up on a whim.'

'Do you have a secret longing to be an artist, then?'

'It's even cornier than that. You know my surname's Williams. Well, my mum's nuts about the watercolours done by that Welsh chap, Kyffin Williams. No relation. Mum's going to be fifty soon, so I thought I'd do her a watercolour as a birthday present. It'll be a watercolour from a different Williams.'

'That's a really lovely idea, Nick.'

He exaggerated an affronted expression. 'You don't have to sound so surprised.'

She laughed. 'I'm sorry. And have you enjoyed the week so far, apart from the Clare bit? You can be honest. Every bit of feedback is helpful.'

'Funnily enough, I have enjoyed it on the whole. But I wouldn't go on another course like this again – it's not really me. By the end of the week, though, I'll have a present for Mum, and I'll have done something different. Yeah, I guess it's been all right.' The sound of approaching voices came from within the house. 'Don't tell anyone why I came on the course, will you?' he added quickly. 'I'd lose all credibility.'

'Of course, I won't. Your terrible secret's safe with me,' she said, glancing towards the patio doors. 'We're about to be joined by the honeymoon couple, I suspect.'

'Now they're something else,' he said. 'I can't see how Howard can put up with that ghastly woman. She always seems to be playing a part, and what's more, playing it badly. I don't know about love being blind, but it's certainly deaf in Howard's case.'

'Shush, Nick.' She smiled up at Paula and Howard as they came up to the table. 'Hello, you two.'

Nick stood up. 'I'm on drinks duty this evening. Take a seat and I'll get you your poison.'

'Ooh, thank you, Nick; that's very sweet of you.' Paula sat down next to Jenny. 'Wasn't it a simply lovely day today?'

'I'm glad you enjoyed it.'

'Oh, I did.'

'We both did,' Howard called as he strolled over to the display of watercolours and began to look at them.

A few minutes later, Nick returned with the drinks. He gave one to Paula, took the other over to Howard, and then sat down opposite Jenny and Paula. 'So what did you get up to in Assisi, Paula? I didn't see you and Howard at all today, and it's not that big a town.'

'We've been to Assisi once before,' Howard said, leaving the paintings and coming to sit next to Paula. He put his arm around her. 'We'd just got engaged the last time. We weren't there for long, but it was long enough to do all the touristy things, like see the Church of St Francis. So today we did the not-so-touristy things.'

'Such as?' Nick asked.

'Mainly wandering through the narrow medieval streets at the top end of town. There aren't as many tourists up there. We photographed all the places we thought would make good pictures, pottered around for a bit, and finally ended up in the main *piazza* and had coffee. Oh, and Paula bought one or two things.'

'I didn't realise you'd been to Umbria before,' Jenny said in surprise. 'How long were you here?'

'Not long; less than a week,' Paula replied. 'We were on a whirlwind coach tour of the highlights of Tuscany and Umbria. It was only a short tour, but it was absolutely wonderful.'

Howard nodded his agreement. 'We liked what we saw of Assisi – they did a brilliant job of restoring it after the earthquake. In fact, we thought the whole area beautiful, and marked it down as a place worth spending some time in. And then we saw the art course advertised, and Bob's your uncle.'

'It's certainly an unusual sort of honeymoon – not coming to Umbria, but going on a course like this.' Nick fetched another bottle of Prosecco from the side table and topped up all of their glasses.

'We like being active, don't we, Howie? It's boring doing nothing. We've got friends who've honeymooned in places like the Bahamas, but that's not for us. This is much more fun, and when we get back to England, we'll be able to show our friends not only the photos we took, but also the watercolours we've done.'

'Riveting stuff,' Nick muttered under his breath. Jenny sent him a warning frown. He winked at her and returned the bottle of wine to the ice.

'Are you flying back to England at the end of the week or are you going on to somewhere else first?' Jenny asked, turning back to Paula and Howard.

'We've got a flight booked for a week on Saturday,' Howard told her. 'We're going to hire a car for a week and drive from here to the area around Arezzo. When we come across an interesting-looking place, we'll find an *agritourismo* and stay the night.'

'Which is why we're travelling light,' Paula said. 'Mind you, it was difficult getting everything into one case. Howie was very strict with me,' she added with a giggle. 'But we need to be able to fit everything into the boot of the car so we don't leave anything on show. Not that I need any more than that – not when I have my Howie with me.' She gazed adoringly at her husband.

'So that's why you were talking to the car hire man, the one from the place next to the internet café,' Nick said.

Howard's hand slipped from Paula's shoulder. He straightened up. 'What are you talking about?'

'Clare saw you talking to him when we were in Montefalco on Sunday.'

Paula leaned closer to Howard and nestled up to him. 'Yes,' she trilled. 'But he charges too much. We're making other arrangements. That's one of the reasons why we'd like to use the internet.'

'How come you were able to understand the man?' Nick asked. 'I didn't think he spoke English.'

'Don't you believe it. Most people in a business like that

speak a bit of English,' Howard said with a laugh, 'but some like to pretend they don't. They get sick of tourists coming to Italy and expecting everyone to speak their language; and I don't blame them, to be honest. I know that Paula and I are among the worst offenders, but we're definitely going to make a start on learning Italian before we come again.' He looked towards the house. 'The others are taking their time. I suppose we could …'

'Here we are,' Clare called cheerfully, appearing round the side of the house with Stephen at her side.

'Where did you come from?' Howard asked.

'Stephen wanted me to see Max's house.' Clare beamed. 'We had a cup of tea with Max on the *loggia*, and then Stephen and I went for a short walk around the garden. It's really lovely there.'

Howard and Paula exchanged glances.

'Your uncle said we could use the internet, Stephen,' Howard began. 'He said that at dinner the other evening.'

'And that we could take a peek at his paintings at the same time. Not the ones he did himself,' Paula giggled, 'but the ones he's got on his walls. Do you think it'd be all right if we popped across now?' She glanced at her watch. 'There's still plenty of time before dinner. We wouldn't be long.'

Stephen looked worried. 'Now's not really a very good time. When we went off for our walk, Uncle Max went for a shower, and then he was going to come over and join us. I think he'll be here pretty soon. Why don't you wait till he gets here, and then ask him if you can go across tomorrow?'

'What's this about tomorrow?' Max asked, coming up behind Stephen and Clare.

Nick's remark about the way she and Max kept staring at each other jumped into Jenny's mind. Her eyes involuntarily flew to Max's face, and she blushed. She hastily bent down to adjust her sandal, hoping that no one would notice.

'I didn't realise you were only just behind us,' Stephen told Max. 'You should have called out and we would've waited for you.'

'You didn't exactly look as if you were anxious for company,' Max replied. He glanced at Stephen and Clare in amusement.

Howard half rose from his chair. 'I was asking Stephen about the internet, Max. Paula and I were wondering if we could check our e-mails tomorrow morning, and perhaps use the internet for one or two things after that.'

'And maybe have a little look at your paintings at the same time,' Paula added. She gave Max a coy smile.

'Pass the sick bucket,' Nick muttered into his drink.

'I don't see why not, providing that it fits in with the plans for tomorrow. What *are* tomorrow's plans, Jenny?'

'I've moved the optional visit to the vineyard from tomorrow afternoon to Friday. We did a lot of travelling today and I thought we should have a rest tomorrow. The plan's to stay here and put together the sketches and ideas we've been working on. Then we're going to talk about how we could use them as the basis for a larger, more ambitious project. As far as tomorrow evening goes, I've booked dinner at a restaurant in Montefalco. Carlo's going to drive us there.'

Max smiled. 'It sounds the perfect day.'

'Does that mean that you're joining us tomorrow?' she asked with a smile.

'It does indeed. By staying at home today, I've been able to catch up with everything urgent, and I can give myself a break tomorrow.' He turned to Howard. 'Why don't you and Paula come across straight after breakfast? Use the computer and then have a look at my pictures. I'm sure it won't take long.'

'That's so kind of you, Max; isn't it, Howie?' Paula sighed.

'Paula's right, it's very sporting of you, Max. We both—' Howard's words were drowned by a loud crash.

They all turned sharply. George was standing at the edge of the terrace, staring helplessly down at the two framed pictures he'd knocked over.

'Oh, dear me,' he said. 'I do apologise – so very careless of me.' Stephen rushed forward and picked up the paintings. 'Thank you, dear boy. So kind. How clumsy of me.' He looked apologetically at them. 'I'm afraid that once again, I'm guilty of sleeping for too long.'

Jenny got up, went over to him, put her hand gently under his elbow and led him to the table. 'There's no such thing as sleeping too long, George. If you're tired, you need to rest. It's as simple as that. We've walked a long way today, and it's hardly surprising that you're exhausted. I know I am.'

She helped him into his chair.

'How kind you are, Jennifer. Thank you.'

Nick put a drink on the table in front of him. 'That'll get you going again,' he said cheerfully.

'Thank you, Nicholas.'

'Did you like what you saw of Assisi, George?' Max asked, pulling out a chair and sitting down next to him.

'I did, indeed. It's a truly beautiful town. I must confess, though, that the hills make it difficult for someone like me with old bones to get around. I did, however, manage the short walk down to the Basilica of San Francesco, steep though it was.'

'That's quite a walk,' Max said. 'Even on a cool day.'

'I was keen to look at the church's architecture, but there was a service about to start, so I decided not to go in until afterwards. Instead, I sat in the sun and watched what was going on. The courtyard was a sight to behold. Hundreds of priests in white robes and red caps were milling around in front of the church, and then they started filing into the church in pairs, singing as they went. What with the sun shining brightly, the bells chiming and the priests chanting, it was all highly evocative.'

'I wish I'd seen it,' Clare exclaimed.

'Indeed, it was quite moving, Clare. I watched until the

very last priest had gone inside, and then I went to find some lunch. By the time I'd finished the lightest *gnocchi* I'd ever tasted, followed by goose breasts sliced as finely as *prosciutto*, and enjoyed a crisp white Orvieto, I'm afraid that I'd rather forgotten about the church's architecture, and I made my way back to the *piazza*.'

He smiled ruefully around the table.

'It sounds as if you've had a very exciting day, Mr Rayburn. Now I wish we'd gone to see the church again,' Howard remarked.

'It does sound an interesting experience,' Jenny said. 'What a shame I missed it. Ah, here's Maria. It looks as if our meal is on the way. I hope you've left some room for your dinner, George. We'll need all our creative skills tomorrow, and a good meal tonight will help.'

She included Max in the wide smile she gave the small group. He smiled back at her.

Nick's words sprang again to the fore of her mind, and she quickly went to the end of the table furthest away from Max.

With the meal finished and the group on the way to their beds, Jenny stared along the deserted table at Max, who showed no inclination to move.

'I'm not surprised that they've all turned in so early this evening,' she said, playing nervously with her empty glass. 'I think we're all pretty much worn out after our day in Assisi.'

'Well, if you're tired, you certainly don't look it,' he said, and he got up and came and sat next to her. She inhaled the smell of him, the muskiness of his pine aftershave, the heat of his skin, and she shivered.

'I missed you today, Jenny,' he said softly. 'All day long, I kept wondering what you were doing.'

She tried to laugh. 'You knew what we'd be doing – you've got the programme for the week and you've got the breakdown for today.'

'So I have. Silly me.' He gave her a slow, lazy smile.

A frisson of excitement ran through her, curling her toes.

She knew that she ought to get up and go to bed. To be alone with Max on a balmy evening in a spotlit garden, the air filled with the heady fragrance of the fading day; just the two of them alone beneath the glittering stars and the fairy lights that twinkled in the leaves above, it was asking for trouble. It would be oh, so easy to lose her focus, to forget the past and give in to the longing that was surging through her. Much too easy.

But she mustn't; she couldn't. Not even if she wanted to, and she didn't; she really didn't.

It was just that him being so close to her made her feel things she didn't want to feel. She hated the fact that she was aching for him; that she was longing for him to put his arms around her and pull her close to him; that she was yearning to slide her hand beneath his shirt and run her fingers across the lean muscle of his chest. Hated the fact that she felt weak with desire at the thought of his body hard against hers, of his touch on …

She shouldn't want that. Not with him. Not with the man who helped to destroy her father. She could never lose her heart to someone who'd done what he'd done. What would that make her?

And how could she even think about taking advantage of his feelings for her, knowing that he liked her? What sort of person did that?

But she had to be that sort of person. She had no choice: it was the reason she'd come to Italy; it was what she had to do.

But not that evening. Not after a long day in Assisi, when she wasn't sure she'd have the strength to keep her distance. She'd do what she had to the following day. She'd need a clear mind if she was going to find out anything, and her mind was far from clear at that moment.

He moved closer.

She couldn't breathe.

She jumped up and stepped back from the table. 'To be honest, I feel shattered. I'll see you tomorrow, Max.' She paused a moment. 'I'm very much looking forward to it,' she added. She forced a smiled to her lips that promised much, then turned away fast.

But not so fast that she missed the look of pleasure that spread across his face.

Chapter Ten

Jenny jumped out of her bed, went over to the window and threw open the shutters. The air was alive with the sound of birds singing and distant dogs barking. Sunshine spilled on to the stone floor of her room, bathing her in the bright morning light. Leaning forward, she rested her elbows on the narrow windowsill and stared at the view.

Framed by the window, lush green grass was bordered by a low wooden trellis around which white-petalled roses curled. Beyond the trellis, the grass stretched away to the rim of the slope, its verdant green spattered with colour from the wild flowers that grew among its blades. The steep descent of the olive trees down the slope to the plain below was marked by their feathery tips, which reached up to the clear blue sky.

It was a scene that she absolutely had to capture in watercolour before she left Umbria.

She turned round to face her room, leaned back against the window sill and stared round her in a mixture of trepidation and excitement. The previous day, she and Max had taken a step forward in their relationship: they'd moved from being merely an employer and employee, to being friends. Admittedly, it was a friendship with romantic undertones, which she hadn't sought and didn't want, but it had brought her closer to achieving her goal.

She had no idea how she was going to make the leap from friendly banter to a discussion about wrongdoing in the past, and that was scary. She'd have to hope that at some point Max would say something she could use to lead him back to the past. Maybe he'd make some further comments about Peter, and she could remind him of what he'd said the day before and ask him what he'd meant.

At the same time, she'd have to do her best not to encourage him romantically. It wouldn't be fair on him.

And as for her … She couldn't pretend to herself any longer that she didn't have feelings for him – she did.

If circumstances were different; if she didn't have to keep holding herself in check, reminding herself why she was there and that Max's charming, friendly face was merely a front for a very different sort of man; if it weren't for this, she'd be free to give in to the way she felt, to do what she wanted to do – her knees felt weak …

She glanced across the room at the clock next to her bed, and promptly straightened up in horror.

Damn, she thought; it was much later than she'd realised. She'd wanted to finish her breakfast before Paula and Howard appeared on the terrace, but it was too late now to get ahead of them. How stupid of her!

The moment she'd lain back on the pillow the night before, it had hit her that if she went across to Max's with the Andersons, she might be able to look round a room or two whilst he was showing them his computer.

She couldn't believe that she'd almost missed seeing how she could turn the situation to her advantage. It just showed how easily an emotional involvement with Max could make her lose her focus.

There'd almost certainly be some photos on display at his house, and these would give her an excuse to go back to the conversation about his family and their business, and from there she could introduce the subject of her father. It hadn't seemed the right time when they were in Bevagna, but she'd have to tell Max who her father was at some point if she was going to get any answers, and this could be as good a time as any. In fact, it would be a relief to get it over and done with.

Her last thoughts before she'd fallen asleep had been that she'd get up early, have breakfast on the terrace and then wait for the Andersons to arrive. She'd tell them that she was going to go to Max's with them as she was curious to see his paintings too.

But they could have already gone by now.

She hurried into her bathroom and showered at speed. Then she put on her sky-blue halter-neck sundress, brushed her hair and clipped it on top of her head with a tortoiseshell comb, slipped into silver low-heeled sandals, and rapidly made her way to the terrace.

It was empty. Paula and Howard were either eating breakfast alone, or they'd already gone across to Max's.

She hesitated next to the buffet table, not sure what to do.

She could always hang around for a while to see if they appeared, but if she did, she'd run the risk of getting trapped in conversation with the next person to arrive, and she didn't want that. If they'd already gone to Max's, she needed to get there while they were still using the computer.

'*Buon giorno.*' Maria came on to the terrace with a pot of coffee and a jug of fresh milk. She put them on the table and turned to leave, but Jenny called to her and asked if the Andersons had had their breakfast yet.

They'd asked to eat a little earlier that day, Maria told her. They'd finished already and gone out. But it wasn't long ago – it couldn't have been more than a few minutes.

That decided her – it would take them some time to check their e-mails and find a hire car, let alone look at Max's paintings, so she'd have time to grab a bowl of cereal and a quick coffee.

She tipped some flakes into a bowl, added milk, picked up her spoon and went and sat down.

'Good morning, Jennifer. Or should I say *Buon giorno*?'

She groaned inwardly, and looked up. George was approaching the table, a wide smile on his face.

Damn. Why must this be the first morning that he hadn't overslept?

He took the place opposite her. 'What a glorious day this is. Painting in the garden is going to be most pleasant after our exertions of yesterday.'

'It is a lovely day, isn't it? Can I get you anything,

George? Some cereal maybe, or a piece of cake? I know you don't like cheese in the morning.'

'Indeed, I think I shall have some cake this morning, but not until I've had my cup of tea. I find that I'm getting quite used to the Italian breakfast.'

'I suspect you're the only one. I still prefer cereal and I'm sure the others do, too.'

A moment later, Maria came out with hot water and tea bags, which she put next to George. Jenny started to eat her cereal quickly.

'You seem to be in a hurry, dear lady,' George observed.

'I am.' She finished the cereal, picked up her coffee and gulped it down. 'I'm afraid I'm going to have to ask you to excuse me. I want to get over to Max's while the Andersons are still there, and I'm not sure how much longer they'll be. Like Paula, I'm keen to see his paintings, and it suddenly occurred to me that it would be less invasive to do so at the same time as they did.'

'How thoughtful, my dear. Nevertheless, I'm sure that he'd be delighted to show them to you at any time.'

She glanced across the table at him. His eyes were twinkling.

She looked at him suspiciously. 'What are you trying to say, Mr Rayburn?'

'That I rather suspect he'd prefer to show you his paintings when the two of you were by yourselves.'

'This is about the paintings and nothing else,' she said firmly.

'Of course it is. Why else would you want to visit the home of a delightful man, who clearly finds you quite delightful, too?'

She forced a laugh and stood up. 'You and Nick are as bad as each other, and you're both wrong. I won't be long – after all, it's only a small collection. You can make a start on your work when you've finished eating, if you want. Would you tell the others that, please?'

She hurried across the terrace and made her way up the

side of the house to the path that ran between the cypress trees, linking their garden with Max's. She half ran along the path, but slowed to a fast walk when she came out on to the lawn in case anyone should be looking out of the windows.

Glancing to her left as she made her way across the grass, she was relieved to see that the wrought-iron gates at the top of the wide drive leading to both of the houses were still locked. A heavy padlocked chain was coiled around the two gates, holding them together. Max was obviously still in the house and hadn't decided to go off anywhere while Paula and Howard were sorting out their e-mails.

As she drew near to the *loggia*, she saw that the French windows at the back of the house were open, suggesting that Howard and Paula had gone in that way. She'd go around to the front, she decided. She knew that Stephen used the French windows for convenience and she was certain that Max wouldn't mind if she followed his example, but it wouldn't feel right.

She walked past the stone pillars that supported the *loggia* roof; clusters of pink roses were growing around each of the pillars, and she leaned across to smell them. At that moment, Stephen came bounding through the French windows.

He glanced in her direction, and stopped short.

'Jenny! What a surprise. I was just coming over to join you all. I decided to have breakfast with the others today. D'you know where you're going or d'you want me to take you to the old man?'

She straightened up and took a few steps towards him.

'I'm fine, thanks, Stephen. I was just going round to the front. I've come across to check on Paula and Howard. They said they were going to try and hire a car for Saturday, and it occurred to me that they might need some help with the Italian,' she added with a flash of inspiration.

'They seem to be doing all right, as far as I can tell.

Howard's on the internet and Paula's having a guided tour of the place. Go in this way. Uncle Max and I always do.'

'Thanks,' she said and she started walking towards the open doors.

'Well, if you're sure that you're OK and you don't mind going in on your own …'

'You get off, Stephen – you don't want to keep Clare waiting,' she laughed. 'But thanks for the offer.'

'I'll see you later, then.' He grinned, gave her a little wave and started to run across to the cypress trees.

She went up to the French windows, hesitated a moment, and then went through them into the house. Pausing, she looked around her at what was obviously a sitting room. Whoever had planned the interior design had managed to make the room look comfortable and, at the same time, stylish. Quite an achievement, she thought.

When she'd gone a little further into the room, her gaze fell upon a huge oil painting hanging above the fireplace. She stared up at it, mesmerised. The painting was a stunning blend of greens on a stone-coloured background, absolutely perfect for its position in the room, and a fascinating exercise in colour.

With great difficulty, she tore her eyes away from it, telling herself that she was meant to be looking for photographs, and she continued to look round the room. And then she saw what she was looking for. Three silver-framed photographs stood on a slender mahogany table next to the wall. Even from where she was standing, she could tell that they were informal family-type photographs, and she quickly went over to them.

The first was of a very young Stephen. He was leaning against a dark-haired woman, who was smiling down at him. That must be his mother, she thought. The other two were of the same man – Peter. There was no mistaking the face that she'd first seen on the obituary. In the first of the two photos, Peter was by himself, staring into the camera.

In the other, he had his arm round Max's shoulders and they were standing in front of a large warehouse. Max couldn't have been more than about fifteen or sixteen at the time.

She picked up the photo and peered at it.

'And in here you'll see the painting that I had commissioned in London earlier this year. It's by one of my favourite artists.' Max's voice came from just outside the sitting room door.

She stood rooted to the spot, unable to move, the photo in her hand. The door opened and Max came into the room, closely followed by Paula.

'Just have a look at this, Paula. It's ... Jenny!' he exclaimed. His face broke into a broad smile and he took a step towards her. 'What a lovely surprise.'

Paula spun round to face her. For a moment Jenny thought she saw anger flash across her face, but the moment passed and Paula was smiling brightly. She must have been mistaken, she thought.

'You should have told us you wanted to come across, too, Jenny,' Paula said. 'We would have waited for you. Silly you.' She gave her little-girl laugh. But Paula's bright smile didn't quite reach her eyes, she noticed.

She suddenly realised that Paula would have wanted Max's undivided attention while he showed her his collection. No wonder she was annoyed to see her there. Upon reflection, she shouldn't have invited herself along in the way that she had, and certainly not without asking the Andersons in advance. However, it was done now, and she'd have to brave it out.

She put the photograph back down on the table.

'I'm sorry for barging in on you like this,' she said, moving over to them. 'It was a sudden afterthought. When I woke up, I remembered that you were going to hire a car, Paula, and I thought you might like some help with the Italian.'

'We didn't have any problems, thank you. You can

get an English translation online, or book through an English website – that's what we did. But thank you for the thought, anyway,' she added.

Turning her back on Jenny, she started to look round the room, and then stopped. 'Oh, Max,' she cried, pointing to the painting that hung above the fireplace. 'Is that the painting you had commissioned?' She moved closer to it. 'It has such feeling to it, such movement.'

'That's the one. And that completes my collection, such as it is.'

Paula glanced at him over her shoulder. 'It's a wonderful collection. Truly it is,' she said tremulously. 'What a thrill to be surrounded by such beauty every day. Don't you think so, Jenny?'

'Yes, I do.'

'But aren't you afraid that people might break in and steal the paintings?' Paula asked, frowning slightly. 'They must be worth a lot. I'd be so frightened that I wouldn't be able to sleep at night.'

'Not really. It's only a modest collection, and I don't make a point of going round telling people what my hobby is. The windows and gates are locked every night and whenever the house is empty; the place is as safe as Fort Knox. The shutters lock automatically so you don't even have to remember to lock them yourself. No, I don't think anyone could get in, even if they wanted to.'

Paula turned back to the oil painting and stared up at it. 'I love all of your pictures, Max, and this one is particularly stunning, but it's my second favourite, not my favourite. My favourite is that darling still life on the landing. I love the effect of the light on the fruit. Why don't you show it to Jenny and see if she agrees with me that it's absolutely the most wonderful thing ever?'

'OK. Jenny,' he said with a smile, 'let's see if your definition of the most wonderful thing ever is the same as Paula's.'

'Whilst you're doing that, Max, I'll go and have a look

at the view from the *loggia*. That's a picture in itself, an ever-changing one.'

'That's fine; go right ahead. Come on, Jenny,' he said, leading the way into the hall. 'And we can see how Howard's getting on whilst we're up there.'

Just as he finished speaking, they heard the sound of Howard clattering down the stairs, two at a time. Seeing them approaching the foot of the stairs, Howard came to a stop on the bottom step.

'You'll find Paula on the *loggia*,' Max said with a smile. 'I hope you got everything done that was on your list.' He made as if to go round Howard, but Howard stayed where he was, slightly blocking the staircase.

'I thought I heard your voice, Jenny. I'm very grateful to you, Max. Yes, mission definitely accomplished. At least, I hope it is.'

'Where does the hope come in?'

'We asked to have the car brought here on Saturday morning, but it turns out that they've got an operative coming to the area today. He's got to pick up a car near here this evening and return it to them. They've asked if he could bring us our car tonight. Apparently, it's cheaper for them if we take it today than if we make them send out someone on Saturday.'

'I don't see what the difficulty is. Of course you must take the car today if that's what they want you to do.'

'Well, I've provisionally agreed. But I wanted to check with you first to see if that was all right. I can change the arrangement if it isn't. The point is, we'd have to bring the car back here this evening so we'd need to have the gates open. We couldn't risk leaving a hired car outside on that narrow road all night.'

'That shouldn't be a problem. What time do you think you'll get the car?'

'I'm not quite sure. We thought we'd go up to Montefalco in the late afternoon, wait for the car, and then bring it back here. If you've already left for the restaurant by the time we get back, we'll dump the car and come up on foot and join you.'

'Well, why not stay in Montefalco if the driver's late getting there? You could go straight to the restaurant and meet us there. Then you could drive the car back after dinner.'

'I was going to do that, but then I realised that I wouldn't be able to have a drink. George has been going on and on about the bottle of wine he's going to treat us to this evening and I'm very keen to try it. That's why I thought we'd leave the car at the house and walk back into town. It'd be a crying shame not to have a drink on our first and last restaurant dinner together.'

'I take your point. Well, how about us moving back our reservation? There must be a limit to how late these drivers work. Then we could all go in the minibus together.'

'That's very sporting of you, Max, but I think it'd be unfair on George. He does so like his routine, even if his habit of oversleeping sends it a bit off course at times. And it would be a shame to have changed the time if the driver arrived earlier than expected. It's more than likely we'll be back with the car long before it's time to leave. But there's just an outside chance that we won't, and that's what I've been worried about.'

'It's not going to be a problem, Howard. What I suggest is, if you're not back by the time we have to set off, we leave the main gates closed, but unlocked. After all, it's not as if it's going to be for very long. But you mustn't forget to padlock them before you come up and join us.'

'We won't. I promise. Thanks a lot, Max.' He threw him a grateful smile. Stepping to the side of the stair, he stared over Jenny's shoulder towards the sitting room. 'I suppose I'd better go and find Paula. It's time we made a start on our work, especially as we'll have to cut short our painting time today. I can't wait to get started on a picture that'll have you reaching for your wallet, Max.'

All three laughed, and Howard left them and went off to find Paula.

'Why don't we leave the still life for another time,' Max suggested, 'and have a coffee now?'

'That sounds very nice, but I don't really think I should. I ought to follow the Andersons' example and get back. I've already been here much longer than I intended.'

He grinned at her. 'I take it that's a yes, then. And so it should be; they'll be fine. You've taught them a huge amount in a week, and it's up to them now to put everything together as they think best. So, let's have that coffee.'

Sitting side by side at a large round table on the *loggia*, they stared across the garden to the shadowy outline of the distant hills, grey shapes veiled in the last traces of the morning mist.

'What a view,' Jenny sighed. 'You've got beauty outside your house and beauty inside it, too. I'm not sure you can claim all the credit for the first – apart from buying the house in such a lovely spot, that is – but you can for the second. You've an excellent eye, Max. Your appreciation of line and colour can't be taught: it's something that you're either born with or you're not.'

A look of pleasure swept across his face. 'I've never thought about it like that.'

'I'm being honest. Your paintings are fabulous. Despite you talking it down, the collection's clearly worth something. Anyone who knows anything about art would know that the moment they saw the pictures – but it's an investment based on real appreciation. And the same can be said of your house.'

'Be careful: in a minute, I'll be sacking you and taking over the art classes myself,' he said with a laugh. 'But seriously, I don't think about their value. They're not for sale: they're for me to enjoy, not for me to make money from.' He paused, and glanced at her. 'Of course, collecting pictures, as with anything else, is much more fun when you can share your passion with someone else. Wouldn't you agree?'

His dark eyes remained on her face.

She picked up her cup, and put it down again.

She'd no idea why she suddenly felt as nervous as she did about the change in direction of their conversation, about the caress in his tone of voice. After all, this was what she'd hoped for when she'd come to Italy. She should feel triumphant, and be alert and ready to profit from the situation. She shouldn't be feeling lost and confused. But she was.

'Don't you agree, Jenny?' he repeated quietly.

Playing for time while she struggled to overcome her emotional turmoil, she took one of the *amoretti* from a ceramic dish in the centre of the table and started to unwrap it.

'Of course, I do,' she said, directing her attention to the paper wrapper. 'Everything is much better when you can talk about it with a friend.'

He sat back in his chair, and stared hard at her. 'I'm curious about something. Why did you come here this morning? Don't get me wrong – I'm delighted that you did. But why *did* you come?'

She stopped playing with the paper and looked at him, startled. 'I told you. I wanted to help the Andersons with any Italian they needed.'

'Now why don't I believe you? Could it be because I'm certain you know as well as I do that you don't need to speak Italian to hire a car online? I suspect you came over for a totally different reason.' He leaned forward. 'Or do I just want to think that?'

She blushed. 'Believe it or not, it's the truth.'

He straightened up and smiled wryly at her. 'And that's why you were looking at the photos of my family when I found you, is it? Despite the urgency of your desire to help the Andersons, you left them to struggle on without you while you stopped to look at a few snapshots.'

'I was just curious.'

'About what?'

This was it, and she had to give it everything she'd got, even if it meant leading him on in a way that wasn't fair to him. It could be the only way she'd get the truth.

'About what your family looked like.' She glanced up at him from under her eyelashes. 'I haven't met many businessmen before, but I can't believe that there are many like you, with business prowess, a passion for art and real taste. I suppose I wanted to know more about you, and your family seemed the right place to start.'

She let her clear blue eyes linger on his face.

He reached out, took her hand in his and stroked it gently with his index finger. Her insides dissolved into liquid honey. 'That's what I hoped you'd say, because I feel the same about you, Jenny. You must have sensed that; you can't not have done. I want to know everything that there is to know about you, about your family, about the things that made you the lovely person you are.'

She pulled her hand away. His sensuous caress was doing things to her insides, turning them upside down, making her tingle all over, making her want to give in to the way she was feeling, the way she couldn't stop herself from feeling, hard though she tried. But she mustn't: it could never be. She had to keep a conscious distance, even if it didn't look as if she was.

'And I feel the same way about you, Max,' she said, her voice hoarse to her ears, 'although I know I shouldn't. You're the man I work for, and I mustn't let myself forget that, much as I might want to.'

'Isn't that something I should have some say in?' he asked quietly.

She put her hands to her cheeks. They were hot to her touch. She stood up and pushed back her chair. 'Talking of work, I really must get back to the class now. They'll have started on their projects a while ago and I ought to see how they're doing.' She took a step away from the table, and paused. 'I'm sorry, but I've really got to go.'

He nodded. 'I suppose you have,' he said with a rueful

smile. 'I won't see you again till lunch – I'm going to do my drawing project here. There's a wonderful view from my bedroom window, and I intend to sit there and draw what I can see. I'm going to include the window frame, too. It'll be a sort of frame within a frame.'

'How funny: I'm going to paint the view from my window too, even the frame.'

His face broke into a smile of triumph. He stood up and went around the table to her side. 'You see, Jenny, we're kindred spirits, just as I thought. And kindred spirits definitely trumps the boss and employee relationship.'

Her knees trembled. She couldn't move.

'Yes,' he said, raising his hand and gently pushing her hair back from her face. 'We're kindred spirits indeed.'

She looked up into dark brown eyes that were flecked with gold, eyes that were gazing down at her with love. Her power of movement returned, and she spun round and ran towards the cypress trees.

Chapter Eleven

Stephen sighed deeply and rubbed his stomach. 'Do we really have to wait for Howard and Paula to get here, Jenny? I'm starving.'

She glanced at her watch. 'I must say, I thought they'd be here by now.'

'They've probably changed their minds about coming.' Nick's voice was tinged with irritation. 'Two lovebirds in an empty nest – they'll be having a right old time in our absence. Shenanigans in the pool, at the very least.'

Stephen and Clare glanced at each other and giggled.

'I doubt that, Nick,' Jenny said with a smile. She turned to Max, who was sitting next to her. 'Shall we order now, Max? I'm not convinced about the shenanigans part, but it's getting on a bit and Nick might be right about them deciding not to come. I think they'd have got here by now if they were intending to join us.'

George shifted to a more comfortable position in his chair. 'If I may say so, I agree with you, Jennifer. And like Stephen, I certainly feel ready to eat.'

Nick laughed. 'Be honest, Mr Rayburn. It's the wine you can't wait to tuck into.'

'Tucking into the wine is not exactly the way in which I would have expressed it myself, dear boy, but indeed you are right in the sentiment: I *am* looking forward to sampling a very special grape this evening. Pleasant though this Prosecco is, it's no more than a prelude to the main event.'

'I'm quite hungry, too. More than that. If I'm honest, I could eat a horse,' Clare said.

Max smiled at her. 'I think you're unlikely to find that on the menu. But I hope something else will appeal to you.'

'Ha, ha. What a wit you are, Uncle Max,' Stephen said.

'Why thank you, Stephen,' Max said with exaggerated gratitude. 'Your appreciation means a lot to me.'

Jenny picked up her menu. 'That decides it then. We'll order now, and if the Andersons turn up later on, they can order for themselves. I don't know why on earth they didn't stay in Montefalco once they'd collected the car – it would have been so much more sensible. It's not as if Howard drinks a lot. At least, he hasn't this week.'

George gave a sudden exclamation. 'How slow of me. I've just realised that I might be able to benefit from Howard having a car.' He beamed across the table at Jenny. 'The vintner in Montefalco is going to bring a superior Sagrantino for me to taste tomorrow, one that will be considerably better than anything we have this evening.'

She heard Nick snigger. Under the table, she kicked his foot. 'Yes, I do remember,' she said.

'I'd been wondering how to get up here. I didn't really want to ask if Carlo if he would bring me up in the minibus since this is a personal visit ...'

'Oh, but you should,' Jenny cut in. 'He's there to help. And he's on standby for anyone who wants to visit a local vineyard tomorrow afternoon, anyway.'

'That's very kind, dear lady. But Howard having a car solves the problem. I can't imagine that he'd mind running me up to the *piazza* at some point. I can make my own way back. Going downhill is quite a different matter.'

'I'm sure Howard would be delighted to help out, Mr Rayburn,' Jenny said. 'Ah, here comes the waiter with more bread and olives. Right, if we're all ready, we'll order now.'

She ordered *antipasti* for the table and then they each ordered their main courses. Jenny looked around the table. 'It's a real shame that we aren't all here. It's the only dinner that we have out all week.'

'I'm surprised that you didn't pick tomorrow night for the final beanfeast, Friday being the last night and all,' Nick remarked.

'I was going to at first, but in the end I changed my mind.'

'How come? Going out tomorrow would have brought the week to a rousing finale, I would have thought.'

'That's true. But in the end, I thought it better to leave tomorrow evening clear for any last-minute packing. Also, you might want an early night before you embark on a day with a lot of travelling. Not to mention that there'd be less risk of you having to travel with a hangover.'

They all laughed.

'You've got a point there,' Nick said, grinning at George.

'You can take it really easy tomorrow – paint, relax by the pool, read, do whatever you like. If you want, you can visit the vineyard in the afternoon, though I'd be careful how much tasting I did, if I were you. We'll be having more wine with dinner tomorrow evening.'

'You can be sure that I, too, shall exercise moderation,' George remarked, dipping a piece of rustic bread into a mixture of oil and balsamic vinegar.

Nick sniggered.

'I'll need to confirm the time that all of you have to leave for the airport on Saturday,' she went on. 'If I remember rightly, everyone's leaving quite early, so it'd probably be wise to do most of the packing tomorrow. Apart from Paula and Howard, that is. They don't have a flight to catch so they can take their time.'

'You needn't worry about their packing. It's done. Or rather not undone,' Clare said.

Jenny laughed. 'That sounds convoluted. What d'you mean?'

'One of their cases is already packed, or rather not unpacked.'

'How come you know that?' Nick asked. 'Have you been a naughty little nurse and been peeking into the honeymooners' boudoir?'

'Idiot.' Clare pretended to throw a piece of bread at him. 'No, I saw it when I was passing their room this morning, didn't I? It was full to the brim and Paula was kneeling on it, trying to zip it up. I asked if she wanted any help, but she said she was fine. She said they'd only used the things in the other suitcase, but she'd had to open that one as they needed more toothpaste.'

'I wish I'd already packed my suitcase, ready to go,' Nick remarked. 'I hate packing,'

'It's easier packing when you're going home,' Clare said. 'You don't have to think what to take with you like you do when you're going away.'

'Aha, here comes our *antipasti*,' George said, as the waiter appeared, carrying two large round wooden boards. He picked up his napkin and tucked it into the neck of his shirt while the waiter placed the boards in the centre of the table, followed by a basket of fresh bread between the platters.

'Ooh, look at that,' Clare said, gazing at the food in front of them.

'Yes, that does look quite delicious,' George murmured. He leaned forward, his eyes shining as he gazed at the variety of cold cuts, cheeses and grilled vegetables on the board closest to him. He glanced across to the second board, which was filled with a variety of *crostini* and *bruschette*. 'Yes, quite delicious,' he repeated. 'If it weren't a cliché, I'd say that it all looks good enough to eat.'

He smiled around the table in satisfaction.

'Good enough to eat and good enough to paint,' Nick added. 'But preferably not in that order.'

Max pointed to a small white pot at the side of one of the trays. 'That'll be honey. You eat it with the pecorino cheese and often with walnuts. It's an Umbrian speciality. It makes a delicious starter – you should try it.'

'How interesting,' George said, and he helped himself to a couple of pieces of cheese. The others followed suit and also took some of the bread and *antipasti*.

Jenny sat very still, staring at the table with unseeing eyes. Something was niggling away in the back of her mind and she couldn't quite put her finger on it.

One of them had made a comment a few minutes earlier

that had jarred, but it had slipped into the back of her mind, just out of reach, and she couldn't get hold of it. If only she could bring it forward and see what it was. It was something that had struck her as strange when it had been said.

'Come on, Jenny, help yourself. There won't be anything left soon,' Max said, his eyes warm upon her face. 'Here, let me pass you the *bruschette*.'

Smiling her thanks, she took the two nearest to her.

'This *prosciutto* is really yummy,' Clare said, happily. 'But I've got a horrible feeling that I've been a pig and taken too much. If I eat everything on my plate, I'll never have room for my *spaghetti*.'

Stephen put his arm round her shoulder. 'It's a case of your eyes being bigger than your stomach.' He pulled her gently to him and kissed the tip of her nose. 'And what lovely eyes they are. I could drown in them.'

'Yuck.' Nick rolled his eyes in mock disgust. 'You could drown in someone's eyes? Let me guess, you're studying English ...'

'That's it,' Jenny cried out. 'They've only got one suitcase!'

They all stared at her in surprise.

'I'm afraid I don't follow you, dear lady,' George said, leaning across and helping himself to another of the *crostini*.

'Who's only got one suitcase?' Max asked.

'They have – the Andersons. Don't you remember, Nick? You and I were talking yesterday while we were waiting for everyone else to arrive, and then Paula and Howard joined us. They said that they had another week in Italy, and had packed light so they could fit all their luggage in the boot of the hired car.'

Nick stared at her. 'Well, yes, she did say something like that. I wouldn't swear to the details, though. But why does it matter?'

'It probably doesn't. It's just that if they do have only

one case, it means that they've already packed it, although there're almost two more days to go. That's funny, don't you think?'

'So you think she was lying?' Max asked, frowning.

She shook her head. 'There's no reason to lie about something like that. There must be a simple explanation.'

'And I'll tell you what else is funny,' Clare said, 'I saw the corner of that hideous flowery thing she wore one evening sticking out of the suitcase. It didn't really register at the time, but it does now. It means she was definitely lying about the case not being unpacked. And maybe she *was* lying about not speaking Italian. I'm sure the car hire man wasn't speaking English – it's the body language. I tried to kid myself that I was mistaken, but I wasn't.'

George wiped his mouth with his napkin. 'But, dear girl, there's no reason why Paula and Howard would lie about speaking Italian or how many suitcases they had.'

Max put down his knife and fork. 'Actually, there is,' he said slowly, 'if you don't want anyone to know that you're familiar with an area and probably have friends and contacts there. Paula was very keen to see my paintings and virtually bulldozed me into showing her around ...'

'And she asked about your security.' Jenny's words fell out in a rush. 'You told her about the shutter locks, and just after that, she was in the sitting room by herself while we went to look at that still life. At her suggestion. She could have easily disabled the most important locks in the time that she had. Oh, Max.' Her hands flew to her mouth.

'And then Howard kept us standing in the hall while he talked about the hire car,' he added. 'He was alone upstairs for some time, too.'

The blood drained from Jenny's face. 'I know it's virtually impossible to believe, but could they be thieves?'

'It's certainly looking that way, and I'm not going to take any chances,' Max said grimly. He stood up, took his mobile phone from his pocket and held it out to her. 'The number for the police is 112. Will you ring them, explain the situation and ask them to get to the house as fast as they can? Road blocks might be an idea, too.'

She took the phone from him. 'What are you going to do?'

'I'm going across the square to get Carlo,' he said. He glanced at the worried faces around the table. 'There's nothing the rest of you can do, so you might as well stay here and finish your meal.' He took a handful of notes from his wallet and handed them to Stephen. 'I'll leave you in charge of settling up.'

'But—' Clare began.

'No buts. You must all stay here.' He turned to Jenny. 'Except for you, Jenny. I hate to ask you to go anywhere where there might be trouble, but would you come back to the house with me? I might need your help with the police when they arrive. I don't know whether they speak English or not.'

'Of course I'll come with you,' she said, tapping 112 into the phone. 'But I doubt we'll catch them. They'll be long gone by now.'

'Not necessarily,' Max said. 'We left the house later than planned – they won't have dared to make a move until they were absolutely certain we were out of the way and no one would come back for something they'd forgotten. It'll take some time to get the paintings down and stack them in the car without damaging them. Remember there are two houses to do.'

'I hope you're right,' she told Max. '*Polizia*,' she said into the phone.

Stephen leapt to his feet. 'I'm coming, too. No way are you going on your own, Uncle Max. Here, Clare, you take the money.'

'I guess I can do the heroic thing, too.' Nick got up. 'Count me in.'

'Thanks, boys. I appreciate it. I'll see you outside, Jenny.' Max hurried out, closely followed by Stephen and Nick.

She rapidly explained the situation to the police, gave

them the location and told them that they were going back to the house. Then she hung up and bent down to pick up her bag.

As she did so, George pulled his napkin from his shirt and started to stand up.

She saw what he was doing and moved swiftly to his side. 'I know what you're thinking, My Rayburn, but no.' She laid her hand on his arm. 'I'd be really grateful if you stayed here with Clare. I don't want her left on her own, and I definitely don't want her coming with us.'

'But I'm a nurse,' Clare insisted. 'You might need me.'

Jenny tried to laugh. 'I'm sure it won't come to that.' Catching Clare's eye, she inclined her head towards George. Clare sat back, nodding that she'd understood.

'It would help us a lot if you stayed with Clare, Mr Rayburn,' she repeated.

'Well, if you insist, Jennifer,' he said, and sat back down again. 'But if I were a younger man ...' He shook his head regretfully.

'Thank you.' She started to move towards the door.

'You'll see that Carlo comes back for us as soon as it's sorted, won't you?' Clare called after her. 'We'll be worried sick until we know that everything's all right.'

'Don't you worry. We'll be back for you as soon as we can. Whatever Max said, they're probably miles away by now. I doubt we'll ever see them or the paintings again.'

Chapter Twelve

Carlo swung the minibus off the main road and on to the narrow lane leading to Max's house. He dimmed the headlights and slowed his speed to reduce the sound of the engine.

From her seat behind Max and Carlo, Jenny kept her eyes fixed on the windscreen, her heart beating fast as she waited to see the wrought-iron gates that marked the top of the drive. But with the minibus going so slowly, the house seemed to be taking forever to come into view, and she eventually turned to gaze through the side window at the expanse of darkness below.

As her eyes gradually became accustomed to the gloom, she saw that the black mass at the foot of the slope was broken up by pinpoints of light from the numerous houses spread out across the plain towards Bevagna, which lay at the heart of the valley, encircled by its subtly spotlit wall.

She glanced down the side of the hill, frantically hoping to see help on the way.

A line of shining stars was winding sinuously in their direction.

She pressed closer to the window, her breath misting the glass; and yes, the starry lights were definitely coming towards them. She sat back in her seat, weak with relief. 'I think I can see the police,' she said, her voice shaking. 'But they're still quite far away. We'd better stop now or we'll get to the house before they do.'

Max gestured to Carlo to pull into the side, shut down the engine and turn off the lights. The minibus rolled a little way forward and came to a standstill just before the road curved sharply to the left.

Stephen leaned across in front of Jenny and stared down at the moving lights. 'You're right, Jenny. It must be the police. Thank heavens for that.'

Max turned to look at Stephen, Nick and Jenny, his face grim. 'Listen carefully. I don't want any heroics tonight. I'm more than grateful that you want to help, but no one – and that includes me – must take any chances. Pictures are only objects, and objects are nowhere near as important as people. If there's anything we can do safely, we'll do it. But if there isn't, we'll sit tight and let the whole lot get taken; if it hasn't been already, that is. I hope that's quite clear.'

'But there's no need for you to do anything, is there?' Jenny asked, her heart beating fast. 'You might get hurt. The police can do what has to be done, can't they? They'll be here any moment now.'

'Distances are deceptive, especially at night, and I'm not sure how long the police'll be. I'd like to see what's going on at the house, so I'll go on foot from here.' Stephen made a movement. 'By myself, Stephen. I want to see whether or not they're still there. If they are, there's less chance of me being seen if I'm alone.'

'Oh, Max. You'll be really careful, won't you? Promise me.' Her face white with fear, Jenny reached out her arm to him.

He took her hand. 'I'll be very careful, I promise,' he said, his eyes on her face. 'I'm not your hero type. Don't you worry; I'll be back in no time.'

He gave her a reassuring smile, squeezed her hand, then dropped it, slid open the door and jumped down from the minibus. 'No one else goes anywhere,' he called up to them. He ran softly to the bend in the track and disappeared around it.

They stared after him. No one spoke. Fear hung heavily in the air.

After what felt like an eternity, he came running out of the darkness. There was a collective sigh of relief the moment they saw him.

'They're still there,' he told them in a low voice as he climbed back in. 'The gates are wide open, and the chain and padlock are hanging from one of the gates. There seem to be three of them – the Andersons and a man I didn't recognise.'

'I bet that's the man Clare saw them with,' Stephen said. 'What are they doing?'

'They were putting one of the paintings into the back of a van. From the size of the picture, I think it's the oil from the sitting room, which suggests that they're almost finished. The lights are on in both buildings, so they must have emptied both houses. I imagine that they did the other house first – the van's parked on the grass at the end of the drive now, very close to the *loggia*. You stay put – I'm going to have another look.'

'Don't go, Max. Wait for the police. They must be almost here by now.' Biting her nail, Jenny peered out of the window down the slope. 'I can't see the lights any more so they must be on the hill behind us, and probably close to us. Wait for them, won't you?'

'Don't worry, Jenny. I'll be very quick. I just want to get some idea how close they are to leaving,' he said, and he jumped down and sped into the dark.

Moments later, he was climbing up the steps into the minibus again. 'I was right. They'll be ready to go soon. It looks as if Howard's about to shut the van doors.'

Nick slid to the edge of his seat. 'Then I say we all go in and stop them. Apart from Jenny, of course.'

'Wait.' Max ordered. 'That's not an option: they might have a gun.'

Stephen laughed dismissively. 'Not Paula and Howard.'

'Yes, Paula and Howard. This has been very carefully planned. No way are they innocent honeymooners, acting on the spur of the moment. It takes nerve to do what they're doing, not to mention skill and some knowledge of the art world. They'll need buyers for the pictures, for example. I'm certain this won't be their first theft and they'll know that Italian police are armed, which means that there's a real risk of them having a gun. No one's charging in, but

I've got an idea that could buy us some time. If it works, that is. We'll need to move sharpish, though.'

Jenny twisted round and stared through the rear window. 'I'm sure I can hear police cars. We can leave it to them.'

'I'm not going to risk them getting away before the police arrive, especially as I think I can safely stop them. Or at least slow down their exit.' Max tapped Carlo on the shoulder and gestured for him to follow him. Stephen started to rise from his seat. 'No, Stephen,' he said quickly. 'You and Nick stay here.'

Jenny put her hand to her throat. 'Please, be careful, Max. Remember what you said about playing it safe. If they see you and they've got a gun …' Panic welled up inside her.

'Don't worry, I won't do anything silly.' He gave her a quick smile, and he and Carlo got down from the minibus and ran towards the bend in the road.

Nick moved into the front seat. 'I'm going to ignore what Max said. They might need help.'

Stephen made a move to follow him, took one look at Jenny's terrified face and sat back down again. He squeezed her arm reassuringly. 'They'll be fine, Jenny. They're not stupid, not even Nick. And you're right about the police being close – I can hear them now. Nick and Uncle Max will be back in a minute, you'll see.'

He fell silent. Side by side, they stared into the darkness beyond the windscreen, waiting.

Almost as soon as he'd gone, Nick was back outside the minibus, standing at the foot of the steps.

'Max and Carlo have closed the gates,' he called up to them gleefully. 'Max wrapped the chain around the gates and put the padlock on. The goons in the van were too busy reversing up the slope to notice what was happening. Great stuff. I'm going to—'

He stopped short at the sound of feet running towards them, and clambered quickly into the van.

Panting, Max and Carlo climbed into the minibus,

slammed the doors shut and threw themselves into their seats. Carlo revved the engine, thrust the gearstick into reverse and guided the minibus swiftly backwards, steering it close into the side of the hill.

Behind them, the distant drone of approaching cars grew into a loud roar. Carlo braked hard.

Max turned to face the seats behind him. 'I'm sure Nick's told you what we've done – we saw you there, Nick. We've stopped them from driving out. The main thing now is to make sure that the police can get past us to the house. We don't want to block their way.'

'Do you think that Howard and Paula will ram the gates?' Nick asked.

'They might try, but they won't succeed. The chain's very strong. No, they're more likely to try to shoot the lock open.'

'Suppose they drive down the slope and escape that way.' Stephen stared anxiously at Max.

'A van like that couldn't stay upright on such a steep slope. They'd know that and they'd never risk it. Besides, there are trees all the way down the slope. They wouldn't have a chance.'

'Suppose they come after us with a gun.' Jenny's voice shook.

'They can't get through the gates any more than the van can. What they might do is ditch the van and go down the slope on foot, but it wouldn't be easy in the dark. And if they did that, they'd be going away from us.'

The back of the minibus was suddenly flooded with light. A car screeched to a halt behind them, and another behind that. They turned to look through the rear window and saw two policeman step out of the first car parked behind them. One of them started to walk towards them; the other waited by the side of the car.

Engines sounded, and one behind the other, three more cars edged past the policemen and the minibus, and continued towards the house.

'I forgot, the gates are locked.' Max jumped down from the minibus. 'They'll need the key for the padlock. Will you tell them where I'm going, Jenny?' he called up.

'Of course I will.' She moved forward and climbed out after him. Her heart pounding with fear, she watched till he disappeared round the corner, then she turned to the policeman.

Standing in front of the wide-open wrought-iron gates, Jenny watched Carlo drive off in the minibus. When he was out of sight, she turned and started to walk down the drive and past the van, which had been abandoned by the thieves in the middle of the drive. She paused and glanced inside; there were several large crates, with a number of paintings slotted into each. The oil painting from above the fireplace lay on top of one of the crates, half covered by a rug.

Two men in protective clothing were dusting the inside of the van for fingerprints, while a policeman was standing by, watching them. She went over to the policeman and thanked him for their quick response to the call and for sending out so many men and cars. Their support had been amazing, she said.

He told her there'd recently been a spate of robberies in the area, especially art-related robberies, and they were very keen to catch the perpetrators. As soon as she'd phoned them and told them about a possible theft, they'd realised that they had a chance to catch the criminals red-handed and they'd thrown everything they had behind it.

They'd also set up two road blocks, he added, one just before the divide in the Bevagna road and the other at the entrance to Montefalco. And just in case the thieves decided to make a run for it, there were handlers and dogs at the foot of the slope.

She thanked him again, and continued making her way down to Max, who was standing at the bottom of the drive, staring towards the end of the garden, which was flooded with bright light thrown out by giant lamps. Stephen and

Nick had gone across the grass and were standing as close to the top of the slope as the police would allow, two black figures, stark against the white light.

She told Max what the policeman had said.

He looked down at her, and took her hand. 'It's just a matter of waiting, then. They won't be able to get far. It'll all be over soon.'

'Thank goodness Clare spotted that they'd already packed,' she said, 'and that Paula slipped up about the suitcases. If it hadn't been for that, they'd have got away with it.'

Just as she finished speaking, they saw two figures appear over the top of the slope, caught in the beam of one of the lamps. Stephen and Nick gave a shout of triumph and jumped up and down on the spot.

Max's hand tightened around hers. 'Here's the first of them.'

'It's Howard,' she said.

The slim policeman walking at his side was beaming with pride. Howard's face was an angry scowl.

Jenny heard a nearby policemen say something to his colleague.

'Apparently that policeman's a champion runner,' she relayed to Max. 'We're very lucky that he was on duty tonight. Anyone racing against him didn't stand a chance.'

In silence, they watched Howard being led past them, his eyes firmly fixed on the ground. Looking back at him, they saw he was in handcuffs. The slim officer propelled him towards the nearest car and indicated that he should get into the back seat.

Max dropped Jenny's hand. 'It's no good. I'd really like a quick word with Howard. Will you ask the officer if I can speak to him? I only want a minute.'

Jenny ran up to the police officer and put Max's request to him. The officer glanced across at Max, then at Jenny, and nodded. Pulling Howard away from the car, he gestured for Max to come over.

He walked straight up to Howard, who turned towards him, his face impassive.

'Why, Howard?' he asked quietly, coming to a stop in front of him. 'Why did you do it?'

The corner of Howard's mouth twisted into a sneer. 'I would have thought that the answer's fairly obvious. Redistribution of wealth, of course. From someone who's got money enough to waste it on expensive ornaments, to someone who needs enough money to buy necessities. It's not that difficult to work out if you look beyond your privileged world.'

'So you're stealing for the necessities of life, are you? Don't make me laugh – you're a common thief. I've worked very hard for everything I've got. But you, you're trying to live off the fruit of my labour, and the labour of others. If you genuinely needed money and couldn't earn it like everyone else, you could have tried asking for help.'

'What, go cap in hand to you and your ilk, begging for a handout? Ask you to throw us some crumbs out of the goodness of your hearts?' His voice rose and he laughed in derision. 'I don't think so. It's a bit beneath my wife and me. Just a bit.'

'And you don't think theft is beneath you?' Max said, contempt in his voice.

'Are you and Paula really on your honeymoon?' Jenny asked, coming to stand next to Max.

Howard laughed even more loudly. 'If you think that, then you're even more gullible than I thought, and that's saying something. Now, if there's nothing else ...'

He spat on the ground, shrugged the policeman's hand off his shoulder, turned and got into the car.

They heard footsteps approaching from behind them, and Jenny turned to see who else they'd caught.

'Look, they've got Paula, too,' she cried gleefully as she saw her being brought up the drive, a policeman on either side of her. One of them had a gun in his hand. 'She and Howard must have made a run for it together. Thank goodness neither got away. Even if the other man did.'

As Paula drew alongside them, she glanced quickly towards the car that Howard was in, and her steps slowed. He looked up at her through the window, gave her a slight smile and shrugged his shoulders. She stopped and turned abruptly to Max and Jenny.

'You pigs,' she hissed, and she threw them a look of pure hatred. 'You filthy pigs.'

One of the officers gave her a push to move her on. Her head held high, she walked forward and let herself be led towards a car that was parked further up the drive.

'Not travelling with Howie-darling, then?' Nick called after her as he and Stephen came running up to stand alongside Max and Jenny.

A loud shout came from the bottom of the garden, followed by the sound of dogs barking in excitement. They spun round and stared down the slope. Two policemen were hugging each other and whooping with delight. Then they gave the thumbs up sign to their colleagues on the drive.

'That must mean they've got the third man,' Max said. 'I'm not surprised – there's no hiding from the dogs.'

A moment later, the head of the third thief appeared above the top of the slope, followed by the rest of his body. As he was led across the grass by a policeman on either side, they saw that the bottoms of his trousers were bloodstained and torn.

Jenny turned to Max. 'It looks as if the dogs got him. He's lucky he wasn't seriously hurt. So now that they've caught the three of them, it really is over, isn't it? I don't think I've ever been so scared in all my life.' Her voice broke.

'My darling Jenny. Yes, it is.' He put his arms around her and pulled her to him.

Encircled by his strong arms, she felt the warmth of his body spread through hers. The fears of the evening faded away, and all memories of the past and why she was there fled from her mind. Thinking only of him, she slid her hands round his back and nestled more closely to him. His arms tightened round her, and all sense of time and place dissolved into nothingness.

'I could stay like this forever,' she whispered, lost in the moment.

'Oh, Jenny,' she heard him murmur into her hair, and she sank deeper into his embrace.

'*Signore.*' A policeman appeared at Max's side. '*Vorrebbe andare in casa con me?*'

'Oh, no, he wants you to go into the house with him,' Jenny translated, her voice muffled by his shirt.

Max sighed, and let his arms fall to his side. Reluctant to do so, she stepped back from him, and for a long moment they stared into each other's eyes.

'*Signore,*' the policeman prompted.

'I suppose I'd better go in and start answering questions,' he said. 'What timing.'

'I'm coming with you.' She moved to his side, and together they followed the officer into the house.

Chapter Thirteen

Breakfast had been a quiet, sombre meal that morning.

Once they'd finished eating, they'd been interviewed in turn by the police, with Jenny translating each time. While the interviews were under way, other officers had searched the Andersons' room and bagged up the few things they'd left behind. Jenny gave them the paintings they'd done, and those had been taken away, too.

By the end of the morning, they'd all felt completely drained, and lunch on the terrace had been as subdued as the breakfast. From the comments she'd heard the police make one to another, she knew that another group was working in Max's house, and that he'd had to stay over there with them, so she wasn't surprised when he didn't turn up to have lunch with them.

'Come on, Clare,' Stephen said briskly when he finished his *panino*. He pushed away his empty plate and stood up. 'I'm not going to let your last full day in Umbria be ruined by the Andersons. We'll go into Montefalco and have our coffee there, and then we'll have a wander around. And we can plan our first meeting in England – it can't come soon enough for me.' He glanced anxiously at Jenny. 'It's OK to disappear now, isn't it, Jenny? I'll go stir crazy if I don't get out for a bit. Clare, too.'

'Of course, it is. You go and make the most of Clare's last day. She hasn't had much fun so far today – none of you have.'

'Are you sure that you don't mind us trotting off and leaving you with the police and everything?' Clare asked hesitantly.

'Of course, I don't.' Jenny smiled warmly at her. 'You go and have a good time. Nothing would give me greater pleasure than to see you enjoying yourselves.'

'Thanks.' Clare jumped up, beaming at Stephen, and they went off, hand in hand.

George rose awkwardly to his feet. 'I find that I am somewhat tired, dear lady, and I think I shall go to my room and have a short lie down. The events of yesterday and today have rather taken it out of me. That's not anyone's fault but Howard and Paula's, mind you, but a few moments of sleep in order to recoup is in order, I feel.'

'That sounds an excellent idea, Mr Rayburn. We'll see you later.'

He nodded to Nick, gave a little bow to Jenny and made his way slowly into the house.

'Right, one of us ought to do some work. I'm going to finish the picture for my mother,' Nick said. 'There's not a lot left to do, and I was tempted to leave the rest till I got home, but I know me – I'd never finish it if I did, and an unfinished picture wouldn't be much of a present for Mother Dearest.' He got up. 'I won't apologise for leaving you alone because I strongly suspect that you'll be delighted to have an afternoon without any of us around. I know that I would, if I were you.'

He gave her a knowing grin, crossed over to his paints and easel, gathered everything together and went off into the garden, whistling.

She sank back into her chair. Nick was right: it was going to be much easier not to have to worry about them that afternoon. George wasn't the only one who was worn out – she felt absolutely shattered. The events of the night, and the words 'My darling Jenny', followed by her total failure to give any thought to what had happened to her father, had gone round and round in her head, and she'd slept only fitfully. To have a relaxing afternoon by herself was an unexpected treat, and a very welcome one.

She sat back. She wasn't going to let herself think about Max; she wasn't going to let herself think about anything at all – there'd be plenty of time for that later. She rested her head on the back of the chair, and stared up at the lilac wisteria that was clinging to the grey stone walls of the house. Very slowly her eyes began to close.

'Where is everyone?' she heard Max ask.

Her eyes flew open and she sat up sharply.

He came up and took the seat opposite her, his face strained and drawn.

'I didn't expect to see you until much later,' she said, pushing her hair back from her face. 'I thought you'd be tied up with the police for longer.'

'They've been there all morning, taking fingerprints and the like. The insurance people are there, too. I had to notify them about what happened. But they can manage without me now, so I came to see you. I didn't expect to find you by yourself, though.'

'Stephen and Clare are in Montefalco; Nick's in the garden, painting; and George is having a rest. We're doing our best to get back to normal, but everyone's still very unsettled.'

'I'm not surprised; it's bound to take a while to get over a shock like that.'

'Have you had lunch?' she asked.

'Just a quick bite – it was all I wanted. What's the state of affairs here with the police?'

'They've taken down all of our statements, and they said they've almost finished. What about you? When they've done everything they have to in your house, will you have to go the station with them? I can come with you if you need me to.'

'I don't think so. They've got my statement, and I've given them Howard and Paula's application forms. What a fiction those were. I can't think what else the police'll need from me. I expect we'll both have to attend the trial, though, and possibly the others, too. If so, I'll pay everyone's expenses. I'm going to refund the cost of the week to them all, anyway. It's the least I can do.'

'That's very kind of you, seeing that it wasn't your fault in any way.'

'That may be. It's a sort of thank you for their support yesterday.' He leaned slightly across the table towards her. At the look in his eyes, her heart gave a sudden lurch.

'And you, Jenny,' he said, his voice warm. 'You were tremendous. I can't thank you enough.'

She gave an awkward laugh and wound a stray strand of hair behind her ear. 'Like everyone else, I was glad to do what I could to help.'

He straightened up. 'Well I want you to know it was much appreciated. As far as tonight's concerned, I've given Maria the rest of the day off. I know she managed lunch, but I think expecting her to cook for us all again today would be too much, and I've booked a restaurant in Bevagna. I thought we'd have an early meal and then everyone can get a good night's sleep. Last night's meal was ruined, and I want them to have an evening to remember before they go home – to remember for all the right reasons, that is.' He gave her a tired smile.

'That sounds perfect. I can't think of a better way of putting last night firmly into the past and enjoying our final night together.'

'That's the idea. I hope it does the trick,' he said, brushing away some wisteria petals that had fallen on to his shoulders.

He glanced upwards as a shower of the lilac-coloured petals, caught by a sudden light breeze, floated gracefully to the ground and rolled over and over across the paving stones, until they came to rest in a heap at the foot of the table legs and around the edges of the patio. The breeze died down and the terrace was still again.

He looked back at her. 'I suspect that it's going to feel very strange to you this time tomorrow with most of them on their way back to England,' he said, leaning forward and pushing aside the petals that had landed on the table in front of him.

She inched her seat back. 'I suppose it will. But it will to you, too. After all, you've joined in all week.' She hesitated a moment. 'Has the Anderson thing made you want to return to England now?'

'Not at all. What happened with them happened, but

it's no more than a blip in what's going to be a lovely summer. It's a blip that's taught me a valuable lesson about security, though, and about what's sensible and what isn't. We'll have internet access over here next year, and there'll be no need for anyone to come across to my place.'

She nodded. 'That's a good idea. It's better to be on the safe side.'

He picked up the teaspoon next to him, and immediately put it down again. 'I think I ought to ask you the question you asked me. It's only fair. Would you prefer to go home now? If you would, you've only got to say. I'd understand – it's been traumatic for you, too. Whatever you choose to do, I'll obviously pay you for the whole of the summer.'

His eyes on the teaspoon, he ran his finger around its rim.

She stared at his bent head. If she went back to England that weekend, went miles away from him, she might never again see him, never again hear him speak, never again feel the warmth of his gaze upon her face, the thrill when his arms were around her. A lump came to her throat. She couldn't not see him again; she just couldn't.

'I'm staying put,' she said, swallowing hard. 'I don't want to leave.'

His shoulders relaxed. He looked at her across the table. 'You don't know how pleased I am to hear you say that,' he said quietly. 'I don't want you to leave. Not at all.'

A wave of relief swept over her.

'So that's agreed,' she said with a half-laugh, tearing her eyes away from his face. 'We're both staying. And now I must go. I've got things to do.'

She went to stand up, but he put his hand on hers to stop her. She sat down again, her stomach jumping nervously.

'I was wondering if you'd say anything about last night, Jenny; not about the theft, but about afterwards, when we were together on the drive. Despite everything that's been going on today, it's been on my mind every minute.'

She pulled her hand away and stood up. 'There's

nothing to say,' she said breathlessly. 'Not now, not ever. I'm sorry; I've got to go.'

He stared up at her, his face puzzled.

'I've got to pick out the best of the week's paintings for this evening's display,' she added, forcing a lightness into her voice. 'We'll make it a bit earlier than usual. And I need to give everyone their work back. At the moment, everything's jumbled together.'

He gestured helplessly with his hands, his palms upturned. 'You don't have to do that now. You could follow George's example and have a rest. You can't have got much sleep last night. We don't need a display tonight – everyone would understand. And they could pick out their own paintings from the pile.'

'I want to do it. It'll help us get back to normal if we start the evening like we always do. It won't be a huge display. I'm only going to show the best of the week's work, and we haven't got the paintings done by two of our number. But I think it'll be enjoyable, looking at the progress everyone's made in a week.'

'More enjoyable in some cases than others, I suspect,' he said wryly.

'Oh, I don't know. I think you're going to be pleasantly surprised at how you and Stephen have improved. You were sceptical, but when you look back at your week's work, you'll see the progress you've made.'

'We shall see.'

'And when we've looked at the paintings, we can have our final Bellini together, and then go out.'

'Fair enough, you've won me round.' He got up. 'I'll leave you to it, then, and get back to the house. Much as I hate the bare walls and the sense of violation, there are things I could be doing there. With luck, the police will have gone by now and I'll be able to get on without interruption. I suggest I come back for seven, in time for the display. The restaurant's booked for eight-thirty, so Carlo will collect us just after eight.'

'That sounds perfect. I'll tell the others when I see them next.'

He took a few steps, stopped and looked back at her. 'I *will* have that conversation with you, Jenny,' he said quietly, 'but at another time. We have the rest of the summer to ourselves, after all.' Then he turned, walked across the terrace and disappeared round the corner of the house.

Her stomach somersaulted. It wasn't *that* conversation she wanted. She wanted to talk about Max and her father, not about Max and her. Not that there *was* a Max and her. There wasn't. Last night, she'd given in to her feelings after a traumatic evening, but it had been no more than that.

Taking a deep breath, she went resolutely into the house and over to the cupboard where she kept the class's work. Kneeling down, she pulled the doors open and took out the paintings and sketches they'd done. Then she pushed the doors shut, sat down on the floor and started to sort them into piles.

A sudden thought hit her hard. She drew her breath in sharply and stared ahead with unseeing eyes. The painting she'd been holding slipped through her fingers to the floor, unnoticed.

She'd turned down the chance to return to England without a second's hesitation. But not for one minute had she reasoned that she must stay close to Max in order to discover the truth about her father. Not for one single second had she cast her mind back to what had happened all those years ago.

All she'd been able to think about was Max and the thought that she might never see him again. And that thought had torn her apart.

She felt the blood drain from her face.

Oh, no, she breathed inwardly. How could she have done such a terrible thing? How could she have let herself fall in love with the man whose actions brought about the death of her father?

Because that's what she'd done – she'd fallen in love with Max.

Chapter Fourteen

Standing beneath a night sky studded with glittering stars, they waved goodbye to Carlo as he drove off to his home, then they made their way slowly down the drive to their house. Behind them, the sound of the minibus engine gradually faded into the distance, until it was swallowed up by the still of the night.

Jenny was the first to reach the terrace.

From the moment she'd let herself face the fact that she'd fallen in love with Max, the rest of the day had passed in a daze, and she'd longed for it to end. She needed time by herself if she was going to get on top of the feelings that she shouldn't have and bring her focus back to the reason she came to Italy.

She could hear Nick just behind her.

'Come on, you slowcoaches,' he called back up the path. He rounded the corner and ran on to the terrace.

'We're going slowly for a reason.' Clare's voice came from somewhere further up the path.

A moment or two later, she turned on to the terrace with Stephen at her side. 'We want to make the most of our last evening in Italy together, don't we, Stephen?' she said, crossing the terrace to join Nick and Jenny. 'When the evening ends, it means that the holiday's ended. We want to delay that moment for as long as possible.'

Nick's face took on an expression of horror. 'For one ghastly minute, I thought you were going to say, "Don't we, Stevie darling?"'

Stephen glared at him, and opened his mouth to speak.

'I thought we'd banned all references, either direct or indirect, to a certain two people,' Jenny cut in quickly.

'Oops. So we did. Mea culpa, and all that,' Nick said, and he hung his head in feigned shame.

She turned to Stephen and Clare and smiled. 'Anyway,

it's not really goodbye for you two, is it? Your uncle tells me that you've been overcome by sudden academic fervour, Stephen, and you've decided to abandon your holiday and return to England to focus on your studies. By a happy coincidence, you'll be able to meet Clare in London at the end of next week. That's right, isn't it?'

Stephen grinned at her.

Clare smiled happily up at Stephen. 'We've been working out all the details.'

'It'll be strange meeting up in England for the first time,' Stephen said, putting his arm round her. 'It's going to make everything much more real. How does it go: Clare's not just for Italy, she's for life?'

Giggling, Clare hugged him.

'Where's Mr Rayburn?' Jenny suddenly asked. She glanced anxiously towards the path. 'I'd better go and check up on him. It should have occurred to me earlier that he might need some help. He looked very tired this evening. I don't know what I was thinking.'

She hurried back across the terrace. As she reached the foot of the path, George came into sight. He was leaning on Max's arm.

'Here I am, Jennifer, as you see. I fear that it's taken me a little longer than sometimes, but I'm here now. Max was good enough to aid me. I am most grateful to you, Max.'

'It was my pleasure, George. Come on, let's get you to a seat.'

Jenny took George's other arm, and they helped him into a chair.

'Thank you, thank you, my friends,' he said, wiping his forehead. He glanced up at Max. 'Yet another reason to be grateful to you, Max.' He glanced at the small group. 'The rest of you may not know ...' Max gestured that he should stop, but George held up his hand. 'No, dear boy, let me speak.' He turned back to the others. 'When the waiter brought us that wonderful wine this evening, it reminded me that I'd completely forgotten the Sagrantino that our friend in Montefalco was going to bring in for me to taste today. As you can imagine, I was beside myself with annoyance that it had slipped my mind.'

'We can, indeed, imagine your consternation,' Nick murmured. Jenny sent him a reproving glance, and he winked at her. She turned back to George.

'Don't worry, Mr Rayburn. He'll know what's been going on,' she said. 'I'm sure the whole of Montefalco will have known about the attempted theft well before the end of the morning. You can go for your tasting session tomorrow before you leave for the airport. You'll easily have enough time.'

'There's no need, Jennifer. Max saw my concern and told me that he'd collected the wine this afternoon and that Carlo had put it in my room whilst we were looking at the display earlier this evening.'

'Oh, how thoughtful of you, Max,' Jenny exclaimed.

George nodded in agreement. 'Indeed, it was. And not just a taste, but a whole bottle of a truly outstanding wine.' He looked up at Max. 'I really am most grateful. Such generosity is overwhelming.' He took a handkerchief from his pocket and wiped first one eye and then the other. 'Quite overwhelming,' he repeated, and he blew his nose.

Jenny glanced around the group. 'Talking of drinks, would anyone like a tea or coffee now, or some wine? Or are you all ready to turn in? It's been a long day.'

'I don't know about the others,' Max said, 'but I'm going to go back now and have a relatively early night.'

'You showing signs of tiredness? You must be ill, Uncle Max.' Stephen started to laugh, but then he suddenly stopped, his expression changing to one of concern. 'Come to think of it, you've been really quiet all evening – not like you at all. *Are* you ill?'

'I'm fine, thanks, Stephen. Everything's rather caught up with me at last. It's nothing serious.'

'I, too, noticed that you've not been your normal self this evening, my friend,' George remarked. 'But that's entirely to be expected. These last two days must have been a serious strain for you. It takes time to recover from such a shock, even for the strongest amongst us.'

'Just so, George,' Max said. 'Right, then, Stephen; time to go, I think. I suggest you say goodnight to Clare and come across with me. Clare's got an early start tomorrow, and I'm sure you'll want to be up in time to see her before she goes.'

Stephen smiled down at Clare. 'I'm going to do better than that – I'm going to wave her off at the airport.'

It was impossible to tell which of them was gazing at the other more adoringly, Jenny thought as she watched them walk along the illuminated path in the direction of the pool, their arms around each other.

'I shall be counting the seconds,' she heard Stephen murmur, and then there was silence.

She heard George give a slight grunt behind her and she turned. He'd put a hand on each arm of the chair and was making as if to rise.

At exactly the same moment, she and Max moved forward to help him.

'I think I shall bid you goodnight,' he said when he was on his feet. 'It's been a wonderful evening, an evening to remember, but I feel more than ready to sleep now.' He nodded briefly to Nick, gave a slight bow to Jenny and allowed Max to help him into the house.

'I suppose I ought to go, too,' Nick said. 'You must be done in, Jenny. I bet you're dying for us all to disappear.'

She forced a welcoming look to her face. 'You said that earlier today, Nick, but you were wrong then and you're wrong now. There's no need for you to go if you don't want to. Would you like a drink of anything?'

'No, thanks. I think I've probably had enough for this evening. I'll be leaving at the same time as Clare and I haven't done any packing yet. I really ought to make a start. So no, nice as it would have been to have had a final drink in the moonlight with you, that would not be a good idea.' He glanced at Max's back and shook his head. 'Shame,' he said ruefully, and then he grinned at her, turned and strolled into the house, his hands in his pockets.

'Ah, there you are,' Max said, coming out of the house as Stephen and Clare came hurrying on to the terrace. Jenny saw that Clare's eyes were red.

Max turned to Clare. 'I probably won't see you tomorrow, but as I'm pretty sure I'll be seeing you again in the future, there's no need for us to say goodbye.' He gave her a warm smile, put his arm round Stephen's shoulders and they started walking towards Max's house, framed by the cypress trees, a row of slender black columns that reached up to the sky, their needle tips silver in the light of the moon.

From time to time Stephen glanced back at Clare, who stared after them until they were lost from sight, then she turned away, her eyes filling with tears.

'Are you all right?' Jenny asked gently.

Clare nodded. 'I'm fine, thanks. Really, I am. It's just that it's been such a wonderful week that I don't want it to end. I've loved everything about it, except for the Anderson thing, of course. But not even that could ruin it for me. I've really enjoyed the painting we've done and I've learnt masses, and I've met Stephen. I can't believe how lucky I am.'

'And he obviously feels the same way. At least, about *you*, he does. I don't know about the painting,' she added with a smile.

'He says he does, but maybe he'll feel differently in England. Maybe the magic will have gone for him. That's what I'm scared about.'

'Maybe he'll feel the same; maybe he won't. Max certainly seems to think that he'll be seeing you again. The best thing for you to do is relax and see what happens. If it's meant to be, it will be.'

'That's good advice, and I'll take it.' Clare wiped her

eyes with the back of her hand. 'And what about you, Jenny? Are you going to take your own advice?'

Jenny looked at her questioningly. 'What do you mean?'

'We've all seen the way that Max looks at you, and we've seen the way you look at him. But then you shut him out. I don't know if you know that you're doing it, but you are. I'm not being rude, but like you said to me, shouldn't you relax and see what happens, so if it's meant to be, it can be?'

Jenny stared at her in surprise. 'Where did that come from?'

'Being a student nurse, you hear all sorts of things. I've heard so many people say they regret not doing things in the past that they'd really wanted to do. By the time that they finally decide to do them, it's nearly always too late for one reason or another. I don't want to be someone who one day, years from now, says "if only". And I don't think you do, either. Or do you?'

'No, you're right. I don't,' she said slowly.

'So go for it. What have you got to lose? Anyway, I've probably said enough, if not too much, so I'll say goodnight now. I'll see you tomorrow.'

With a little wave of farewell, Clare went into the house.

Standing motionless in the middle of the empty terrace, Jenny stared after her.

'No, I don't,' she repeated to herself, and she picked up her bag and made her way back to her room.

Early the following morning, she said goodbye to Nick and Clare at the top of the drive, and a temporary goodbye to Stephen. She waved to them until the minibus was out of sight, and then strolled back down to the house.

So now only George was left, she thought, and not for that much longer. Max was right – it was going to feel very strange when they'd all gone. When it was just her and Max. A wave of ice-cold panic shot through her. Max had made it clear that there were things he intended to say to her, but she was frightened to hear them – she couldn't trust her reactions any more.

Reaching the terrace, she looked around for George, but he was nowhere to be seen. She bit her lip anxiously. She'd have to find something else to do that would take her mind off her fear that Max might materialise at any moment and insist upon the conversation she was dreading.

The class's work. That would do it, she thought in a flash.

They'd taken their best pictures with them, carefully packaged so as not to ruin them on the journey, but she'd photographed them all beforehand, knowing she had some good material there for next year's advertising. She'd deal with the photos later, but first she'd have a look at their earlier sketches and preliminary designs. There was a chance that she could make them into a collage that could be used in some way. If anything could divert her thoughts, it would be that.

She went quickly to the cupboard in which she'd stored their work, pulled out the remaining drawings and spread them out on the floor as close to the patio doors as she could in order to take advantage of the light. Then she knelt on the floor, her back to the glass doors, and started to put the work into piles.

A shadow passed across the room. It stopped in the path of the sun, cutting the stream of light in two.

She swiftly turned to look towards the patio doors.

Max was standing between them, a tall, dark silhouette framed by the bright sun. He stepped into the room and stared down at her, unsmiling.

Chapter Fifteen

He hesitated a moment, then came further into the room.

She scrambled to her feet, brushed the dust from her jeans, and faced him.

'I hope I didn't frighten you,' he said, 'turning up like this. You've gone very pale.'

'You did a bit, to be honest. I thought I was alone, apart from George, of course.'

'Well, you're not alone any longer. I decided to come across and see you.'

Panic welled up inside her. 'I'm not sure where George is at the moment,' she said quickly, 'but he'll be somewhere in the house. I'll pop along and find him, if you want to hang on here.'

'I came to see *you*. You singular. Not you plural.' He took a step forward, then stopped, inches from her. She drew her breath in slowly.

The air hung heavy between them.

She shivered and took a few steps back. 'Why?'

He didn't move. '*Not now*, you said. *Not ever*. Why not ever?'

Her brow wrinkled. 'What do you mean?'

'I can accept the not now: we were both tired at the time. But not the not ever. Why don't you ever want to talk about what passed between us two nights ago? Something did. I felt it, and you felt it, too. I know you did.'

'I don't know what you mean.' Her voice shook.

'Yes, you do. There was something between us, and not for the first time, either. And I keep thinking back to the expression in your eyes when we were in the minibus, waiting for the police to arrive.'

'You're mistaken. I …'

'I don't think I am. At least, I hope I'm not. You were genuinely afraid for me. No one would be that afraid for someone if they didn't have strong feelings for them. They couldn't be.'

Unable to bear the sight of the hope that burned in the depths of his eyes, she looked down at the floor. 'I'd have had the same expression if a litter of puppies had been under threat,' she said weakly.

He gave her a half smile. 'And that would have been a sorry situation, too. But I don't think this had anything to do with puppies. Apart from the fear, I also saw a reflection of what I feel about you.'

Her eyes still rigidly fixed on the patch of floor in front of her, she shrugged her shoulders. 'I don't know what you're talking about.'

'Don't you?' he said quietly. 'Well, let me show you, then.' He put a finger lightly under her chin and raised her face to look into his. She found herself gazing deep into eyes that were dark with longing. Her knees started to tremble. Unable to move, she let out a long, low sigh, and her lips parted.

'This is what I saw, Jenny,' he said, his voice husky. He ran his thumb slowly along her upper lip, then her lower lip, and then he bent his head and lightly brushed his lips across hers.

Her toes curled in pleasure.

A wave of intense desire shot down the length of her body. They couldn't stop at that, she cried inwardly. Without thinking, she reached out to him, and he pulled her to his chest and put his arms around her, his strength enveloping her.

Her every nerve was alive and tingling, crying out to her that she loved him, truly loved him. 'Oh, Max,' she breathed.

For a long moment, he stood still, staring down into her face, then he brought his mouth down hard on hers.

Kissing him back with increasing urgency, increasing desperation, she pressed as close to him as she could, shivering as she felt his body hard against hers. If it weren't for the memory of what Max had done to her father …

Her father!

In a panic, she pulled back from Max, and her hands flew to her face.

'Oh, no, I shouldn't have done that,' she gasped, and she took a step further away from him. 'I should never have done that.'

'Yes, you should have,' he said, his voice caressing her. He went closer to her. His eyes full of love, he gently removed her hands from her face. 'It's what we both feel, what we both want,' he murmured, and he trailed his fingers down her flushed cheeks.

'It's not what *I* want,' she cried, sweeping his hands away. 'At least, I *do* want it, that's the trouble, and I shouldn't.'

His arms fell to his sides. He moved back and stared at her in bewilderment. 'I don't understand. What do you mean, you shouldn't want it? We like each other. You're not in a relationship and nor am I. So why shouldn't you?'

Tears began to roll down her cheeks.

'What is it, Jenny? You're frightening me now.'

Choking on her tears, she shook her head, unable to speak.

'I'm trying to tell you that I love you, darling Jenny. Have I got it wrong, thinking you love me as much as I love you?'

'No. At least, I don't know,' she sobbed. 'I'm completely confused. I can't stop thinking about you. Ever since I met you, it's been one long struggle, trying to stop myself thinking about you, being drawn to you. I think I've got my feelings under control, and then I see you and I know I haven't. I came here hating you, but now I find myself loving you. I can't bear it, but I do. I love you so much, and I mustn't. I can't. I must leave tomorrow. Or even today.'

His face was ashen. 'I don't understand what you're saying. What do you mean you came here hating me? The first time we met was at your interview, so how can you hate me? I know I'd remember if we'd ever met before that.'

She wiped her face with the back of her hands. 'We hadn't met before, not as such. But you've met my father, you and Peter.'

He frowned, and moved back from her. 'What's Peter got to do with any of this? He died years ago. And what do you mean, we met your father? I don't remember ever meeting an O'Connor before I met you.'

'O'Connor's my mother's maiden name. We started using it when we moved to Cornwall after my father died. His name was Francis Egan.'

'Francis Egan?' he said slowly. 'Yes, I *do* remember him. He died in tragic circumstances.' He stared hard at Jenny. 'And you're his daughter?'

She nodded. 'It's thanks to your family he's dead. He was so stressed after a meeting with you all that he drove his car into a wall and was killed outright. I was twelve at the time – too young to lose my father.'

'That's right – he died in a car accident.' Max's brow creased in thought. 'The inquest found that it was suicide. Peter was one of several people questioned at the inquest in connection with your father's financial situation. It was a terrible thing to happen, but I don't know what you mean by saying that it was thanks to my family.'

Jenny's voice rose. 'You were always so late in paying for what you bought from him that he had a serious cash flow problem every month. Because of you and other companies like yours – but mainly your company as you bought so much from him – the bank finally gave up on him and called in his loan. I read what the newspapers said when they reported the coroner's verdict, but they didn't say why you'd made things so hard for him. So why did you?'

'You're wrong about that, Jenny. His death wasn't our fault.'

'It was. If you hadn't paid late … If you'd paid when you should have done … When things were really bad, he even asked you to help him out by paying on time, Mum said, but you refused. You must have seen he was struggling. You knew him, and knew he was a good man – you should have stuck to the contract, but you didn't.'

'You've got it wrong. It wasn't like that.'

'Yes, it was. My mother said that if you'd paid him when you should have done, he'd never have got into such a mess, and he wouldn't have been so seriously stressed that he killed himself. I think that justifies my *thanks to your family*, don't you? So, you see, I won't let myself love you. I can't.'

A loud sob escaped her, and she turned to walk away.

He caught her by the arm. 'But you do love me. I know that, and so do you,' he said bluntly. 'I'm sorry about your father,' he added, his voice softening, 'but you're wrong about the way we behaved towards him.'

She thrust her chin out defiantly. 'If my mother said that's what happened, then that's what happened. Now, let go of me.'

He released his grip on her arm, stared at her for a moment, then turned and went towards the patio doors. He reached them, paused, and then spun round to face her.

'No, I'm not giving up on you that easily,' he said, and he walked back to her. 'I'd never forgive myself if I did. I'm going to clear this up. I have to for both our sakes.'

She stared accusingly up at him. 'Then tell me, why did you and Peter let my father down like that? He looked on you as friends. My mother has never been able to explain that to me or to herself, and we need to know why. That's the reason I came to Italy. All the other things that've happened have just made everything much more confusing.'

'You're confused because you love me, and you think you should hate me. Well, I'm confused, too, Jenny.' She looked at him questioningly. 'I'm confused because I'm in a difficult position.'

'I don't understand. In what way?'

'Well, I've no choice but to defend my family if I'm going to have a chance with you. But to do that, I'd have to say something hurtful about your family, and I don't want to. I love you and I don't want to cause you pain.'

'There's nothing you can say against them.' She heard the angry defiance in her voice. 'They've not done anything wrong,' she added, softening her tone.

'You're right,' he said, his voice gentle. 'They haven't. Your mother told you something that wasn't true, but she acted out of kindness, and it's not wrong to act out of kindness. She wanted to protect you, someone she loved.'

A chill ran through her. 'What do you mean?'

'First of all, we always paid on time – not early, but on time. I believe I actually asked Peter to pay up early on one occasion, but he refused. I admired Peter enormously, but I didn't always agree with what he did, and that was one of those few times. It was rare for us to disagree, and that's probably why I remember the details so clearly.'

She stared at him in surprise. 'Why did he refuse?'

'He said it would merely be delaying the inevitable: your father's business was never going to survive, and giving him a helping hand would only prolong a miserable struggle. I could see what he was saying, but I felt sorry for your father. However, I went along with what Peter said as I figured he knew what he was doing.'

'If only you hadn't given in so easily,' she exclaimed.

'It wouldn't have made any difference, Jenny. Unless every company paid early, your father would still have had a cash flow problem. He had to pay for the goods he bought within four weeks, whereas everyone who bought from him had six weeks to pay.'

'I know that.'

'Your father just didn't have sufficient capital behind him to cover the two weeks' gap. Peter did what he could to help him by regularly paying on time, which is something that doesn't always happen in business.'

She shook her head from side to side, disbelief in her eyes. 'I don't believe it.'

'You can easily check, if you want. Who paid what and when will be in his ledgers. You'll find that your father's financial problems were nothing to do with us.'

'But my mother said …'

'He obviously had too little capital to set up a business on his own, especially a business of that nature. He should have stayed a sales rep, like he was when we first met him. As far as I recall, everyone advised him against going it alone, but I think he was desperate to be his own boss and went ahead, confident that it would somehow work out. And it did for a bit. The local bank manager was probably a friend of his, and as such was sympathetic to your father's problem and turned a blind eye to the two weeks' gap.'

'So why did his business fail?'

'I think the manager was eventually moved to a different branch, as bank managers often are, and the new man was a different kettle of fish. He must have got fed up with your father's cash flow problem, refused to help him through it and finally called in the loan. That's what put your father on the road to bankruptcy.'

'But why did my mother say it was *your* fault?'

He hesitated and then took a deep breath. 'I don't think the collapse of his company was the only strain your father was under. There was something else, too. Please don't hate me for telling you this, but I think your parents were having personal problems.'

'Never,' she whispered. She felt the blood drain from her face.

'I'm sorry, but it's true. Don't blame her too much. She was extremely young when you were born, and they obviously had very little money. It may have been that she felt trapped by everything; I don't know. But whatever it was, she appeared to become infatuated with Peter.'

She gasped in disbelief.

'Believe me, I'm sorry to have to tell you this, Jenny,' he went on, 'but she made a pass at Peter one day when he'd stopped by to see Francis, and Francis was out.'

'She wouldn't have done. And it was never mentioned at the inquest or in the newspapers.'

'I'm afraid she did. But Peter adored his wife and little

boy – Stephen – and he made it clear that he wasn't interested in her. Peter was never asked about your parents' personal life, and I think, perhaps, he didn't want to embarrass your mother by volunteering the information. He was probably a bit more brutal in turning her down than he needed to be; I think he said your mother took it quite badly. Somehow or other, your father found out and I suspect that the stress and fear of losing not only his business, but also the wife and child he loved, was what caused him to kill himself.'

She vigorously shook her head. 'I don't believe you. Mum wouldn't do such a thing – she loved my father and she wouldn't go after someone else, and she certainly wouldn't lie to me.'

'I've told you the truth. Your mother's grief over your father's death was probably mixed up with intense guilt, and perhaps also anger at Peter's rejection. I expect that blaming my family came from a combination of things.'

'I don't believe that of my mother,' she said stiffly. 'She loved my father so much that she still hasn't got over his death. And I don't think she'd lie to me and keep on lying to me. I want you to go now, please.'

Max hesitated, then put his hand in his pocket, took out his mobile phone and set it down on the table next to the wall.

'It's up to you what you do now, Jenny. I can understand you wanting to believe your mother, and it's only right that you should feel that way. But when you've had time to mull things over, if you feel that you'd like to ask her to explain what happened, now that you're old enough to put everything into perspective, then you can use my phone. I'll leave you now, though, since that's clearly what you want.'

He went through the patio doors, across the terrace and out of sight. Not once had he looked back, she realised, as she stared at the place where he'd stood.

'Mum wouldn't have lied to me, she wouldn't. I just don't believe it,' she told herself firmly, sinking to her knees on the floor.

Her words reverberated in the emptiness around her.

Chapter Sixteen

There was a light tap on the door and it opened slightly. Jenny glanced up from her seat on the floor, her face pale and tear-streaked. Hope sprang to her eyes. George's head appeared through the gap, and her heart sank.

He cleared his throat. 'Excuse me, Jennifer. I won't be in your way, will I, if I join you for a few moments? If it's not convenient, however ...'

'Of course, you won't be in the way,' she said flatly. 'Come in.'

As he came into the room, she saw that he looked very tired, and she felt a stab of guilt at how unwelcoming she must have sounded. 'No, do come in, Mr Rayburn – George. I'd be glad of the company,' she added, making a great effort to sound as if she meant it.

'Thank you, dear lady.' He closed the door behind him, went over to one of the armchairs and sat down. 'Please, don't let me interrupt you. I can see that you're busy.' He glanced down at the floor. 'It's hard to believe that we produced so much work in so little time.' He indicated the pictures.

'I know what you mean. You should have seen everything spread out yesterday. It really was quite impressive.' She sat back on her heels. 'To be honest, George, you're not really interrupting anything. I can't seem to get into the right mood today. It must be the Howard and Paula factor. I still can't stop thinking about what they did, or rather what they tried to do. And all the things they said to deceive us. Who would have believed it of them?'

'Who indeed? Nevertheless, in the end you were cleverer than they. It's down to you that they were caught.'

'Down to me?'

'It was you, was it not, who noticed the suitcase

discrepancy? You deserve a pat on the back. You proved to be quite the detective.'

She shook her head. 'I'm not so sure about that. My record for detection isn't exactly hot in other areas. What kind of detective accepts what they're told without question, just because it comes from their mother? Maybe at first they do, but not year after year after year.'

'You are being too hard on yourself, Jennifer. It's understandable to put your trust in someone you love.'

'Well then, what kind of detective doesn't recognise that they're starting to feel too much for someone they shouldn't?' She shook her head and tried to laugh. 'Ignore me, George. I'm just feeling sorry for myself. How are you? Did you get all of your packing done or would you like some help?'

'Everything is done, thank you, apart from the last few things which I shall put into my case just before I leave.' He gave a little cough and shifted his position in the chair. 'I'm afraid that I couldn't help overhearing snippets of the conversation between you and Max,' he said awkwardly. 'I do apologise, dear lady. I didn't want to hear, but I was sitting on the patio in front of my bedroom, enjoying the view, and the doors here were wide open.'

She stared at him in consternation. 'Oh, my goodness, I'm so sorry, George. What must you think of us. Of me particularly. How embarrassing.'

'What I think is completely unimportant. It's what you and Max think that matters. More than that: it's what you both feel.'

'If you heard what we said to each other, then you'll know that I've hated him since I was twelve years old.'

'To be precise, you didn't actually hate Max – you hated what you thought he'd done. There's a great difference, if I may venture to say so. You didn't know Max other than through your mother's words. When you met him and got to know him, you fell in love with the man you found him to be. Now that you know he's innocent of any wrongdoing – and I think you know that in your heart, do you not – you are free to love him. Is that not so?'

She stared at George, and then nodded slowly. 'You're right – deep down, I know Max isn't lying. I trust him completely, and I know he isn't capable of doing something deliberately cruel. But if Max is telling the truth – and I'm sure he is – then my mother isn't, and where does that leave her and me? Even if I could accept that she lied at the time of my father's death, it's hard to believe that she would carry on lying for so long afterwards.'

'Would it not be an idea to call your mother and talk to her?' he suggested. 'It seems unlikely that you will be able to leave matters as they are now, not if you want any peace of mind, that is. Max has left you his telephone expressly for that purpose.'

She glanced towards the mobile phone. 'I suppose I could, couldn't I?' Then she looked back at George. 'But again, it's not that straightforward, is it? If I force her to confess, I'll humiliate her, and I wouldn't want to do that. She *is* my mother, after all, and she's always been a wonderful mother.'

'It is possible, my dear girl, that your mother has been unhappy for years about the lie she'd felt obliged to tell, and to keep on telling. She may welcome a momentary humiliation if it means putting an end to the deception.'

'But no one obliged her to do anything. She could have told me the truth from the very start.'

He raised his eyebrows. 'Indeed? I am trying to imagine how a mother would tell her young daughter, who had just lost her father, that the advances she'd made to another man had added to the father's stress to such an extent that he'd killed himself. It's hard to see how such a revelation could help the daughter in her time of grief, and at a time when all she had left was her mother. No, far better to blame it on someone else, I would have thought. And in this way also make sure that the daughter didn't hold herself responsible for her father's death.'

She stared at him. 'When you put it like that, I can see why she decided to blame the Castaniens at the time. But surely she could have told me the truth when I got older.'

'I suspect that the longer you live with a lie, the harder it is to rectify it. There may never have seemed a right time to come clean, as they say. Nor any reason for her to do so. And your mother may have even come to believe that what she told you was the truth.'

'I suppose that's possible.'

'As Max said, her first thought will have been for you, Jennifer. Don't be too hard on her.'

'What you say does make sense. I can see that,' she said slowly.

'Be that as it may, I am sure that neither what I say, nor what Max has said, will be sufficient. If you're to find the closure you seek, you will have to speak to your mother.' He gestured towards the mobile phone. 'The means to do so is there. And as it so happens,' he said, rising awkwardly to his feet, 'I need to check again that I haven't left anything in the wardrobe. So if you will excuse me, I'll leave you now.'

She jumped up, went quickly to the door and held it open for George.

He started to walk past her, but then paused. 'Listen to your heart, Jennifer; it won't let you down. In your heart you know that Max has spoken the truth; just as in my heart, I know that Agnes would be proud of the progress I've made this week. I did the right thing in taking the holiday she and I planned, even if it was alone.'

'I'm so glad you feel that way. And I'm also very glad that you were sitting where you were and that you overheard what we said.'

'Dear lady,' he said, gently. 'Speak to your mother. When you've done that, you'll be free to go and love your man, and if you have a fraction of the happiness with Max that I had with my Agnes, you're going to be a very happy lady indeed.'

'Thank you, George.' Impulsively, she leaned across and kissed him lightly on the cheek.

Smiling, he inclined his head towards her and went through the doorway into the hall.

She closed the door behind him, leaned back against it for a moment, and then walked over to the table and picked up Max's phone. Her fingers hovered briefly above the keys, and then she tapped out a number she knew by heart.

Chapter Seventeen

The late morning sun was beating down on the garden as Jenny pushed the patio doors wide open and went out on to the terrace. Still clutching the mobile phone in her hand, she stood in the shade beneath the awning and stared around her.

Beneath the deep blue sky, the glossy green and purple sheen of the garden was broken only by the vibrant plants nestling amid the verdant foliage, and by brightly coloured flowers in large terracotta tubs on the terrace.

A light breeze swept across the garden, ruffling the ferns and the bushes. In between the gently swaying fronds, the pool could be glimpsed, its clear water sparkling in the light of the sun.

Breathing in deeply, Jenny inhaled the scent of lavender and rosemary.

What a morning it had been.

It had been achingly difficult to bring up a subject so sensitive with her mother, the person who'd loved and cared for her all of her life and who'd done all that she could to help her fulfil her every dream. At first, her questions had been hesitant and embarrassed, but gradually they'd gathered speed until they were pouring out of her, tumbling one after the other, demanding an answer.

Her mother's initial reaction had been one of shocked surprise, and she'd rushed to deny everything that Max had claimed, insisting that her original account had been the right one.

Jenny'd wanted to stop there, to accept without further question her mother's words and allow her lie to remain, but she couldn't. Her every instinct told her that only by probing more deeply, hateful though it was to do so, would she clear the air and prevent the lie from coming between them.

She'd challenged her mother again. Once more her mother had vigorously begun to deny everything, but all of a sudden, she'd stopped mid-sentence. There'd been a moment's silence, and then she'd started to speak again, her voice somehow different this time, and Jenny had heard from her mother the account that she'd first heard from Max.

From then on, her mother had seemed unable to stop talking, and she'd poured out the whole story amid profuse apologies, and with tears of regret mingled with relief. It was as if Jenny had unlocked the door to something that had been desperate to escape for a very long time.

Her mother hadn't attempted to defend herself – quite the opposite, in fact.

She'd told Jenny that there was nothing she could say that could justify blaming a family who'd acted fairly towards her father. Eaten up by guilt at the time of her husband's death, she'd had the idea blaming the Castaniens in a flash. She'd thought it wouldn't matter what she said as she and Jenny were moving away and were unlikely ever to meet the family again.

Once she'd accused them, she hadn't seen a way of stopping and it had never occurred to her that Jenny might one day seek out the Castaniens. She could see now how wrong she'd been, and that she should have long ago told the truth. She'd finished by begging Jenny to forgive her and not to let their relationship be damaged by the revelations. Then she'd fallen silent, waiting.

'I can understand why you did it,' Jenny had told her. 'And there's nothing to forgive. In your place I probably would have done the same. You acted as you did out of love.' And they had both broken down.

'I've been hating myself for my part in your father's death for so long, and for lying to you the way I've done,' her mother had told her through her tears. 'You don't know how pleased I am that everything's out in the open at last. I feel I can move on now.'

'We both can.'

'I never thought I'd say this, but I'm very glad you went to work for Max Castanien, Jenny. I only saw him once – he must have been about nineteen or twenty – and he seemed a nice lad. What's he like now?'

Jenny bit her lip in sudden anxiety. If her relationship with Max survived their exchange of words that morning, and if it were to develop in the future – a huge if, but she desperately hoped that it would – she couldn't just spring it on her mother without having given her at least some warning.

'Actually, Mum,' she'd begun nervously. 'I ought to—'

But her mother had spoken across her. 'It's all right, Jenny,' she'd said. 'I know you so well that I understand what you're trying to tell me. I'm not saying that it would ever be easy to meet a Castanien again – of course it wouldn't: so many memories are attached to that family. But if he's the right man for you, then you'll have my blessing. It's the very least you deserve.'

'Oh, Mum,' Jenny breathed, and a great wave of relief coursed through her. 'Thank you.'

They'd said goodbye soon after that, both drained of emotion, and she'd wandered on to the terrace in a daze.

Stepping out from under the awning, she put her face up to the sun and let its warmth flow through her. Something tickled her toes and she glanced down. A light breeze was blowing a smattering of white rose petals across her toes. Her eyes followed the petals as they skimmed the surface of the patio and drifted across the grass to the line of cypress trees.

She turned to face the trees and scanned the distance for Max's house. He would be in there now, she knew, and she absolutely had to see him. She had to see him that instant – not the following day, not later that day, but as soon as she possibly could. She found herself taking a step forward, and another, and another.

By the time she reached the trees, she was running.

Not wanting to waste a precious moment by going up the slope to the linking path, she sped through the nearest gap in the line of trees and ran straight across the grass to the *loggia*.

One thought filled her mind, and that thought was Max.

No matter what he felt about her now that he knew why she'd gone to work for him, she had to tell him that she was desperately sorry for what she'd said, for what she'd believed about him, and she had to tell him that she loved him with all her heart. Even if she was too late and her feelings were thrown back in her face, she still had to tell him. He had to know.

By the time she was close to the house, she was panting heavily, and she slowed down to a walk as she reached the *loggia*. The French windows suddenly opened, and Max appeared.

She stopped sharply and took an involuntary step back.

Standing motionless in the shadow thrown by the stone pillar, she followed him with her eyes as he walked to the edge of the *loggia*, his hands in his pockets, and leaned against the column nearest to him, gazing at the view.

He had never looked more handsome, she thought, in his jeans and a black T-shirt, his face and forearms lightly tanned.

And he'd never looked more sad and dejected.

Squinting against the sun, he glanced up at the sky, and then again stared ahead of him.

With a sigh, he straightened up, turned slightly and caught sight of her.

An expression of surprise swept across his face. He pulled his hands from his pockets and took a step towards her.

She stood staring at him, rooted to the spot, her heart racing as he walked towards her, gathering speed with every step, his eyes asking a question.

He reached her and stopped. For a moment neither said a word.

Then she held out his mobile phone. 'I thought I ought to return your phone,' she said, breaking the silence, her voice coming from somewhere far away.

His eyes on her face, he took the phone and put it in his pocket. And waited.

'My mother told me about Peter and her. Not that there ever was a Peter and her.' Her voice caught in her throat. 'I'm so sorry that I blamed you for my father's death.'

'So you *did* call her. I wasn't sure if you would, and I didn't know if she'd tell you the truth if you did.'

'I didn't need to hear what she said to know what had happened – I knew in my heart that what you said was true. But I had to get it all out in the open with her, for the sake of the future ...' Her voice trailed off.

His dark brown eyes gazed down at her, warm with sympathy. 'That's what any loyal daughter would do.'

'I still feel as if I've behaved badly, coming here for the reason I did but not being honest about it.' He made a move as if to speak, but she shook her head. 'No, don't say anything, Max. I must say this while I've got the courage to do it.' She took a deep breath. 'I wouldn't blame you if you hated me, but even if you do, I love you. I love you so much that it hurts. I can't bear to think of life without you. But I'll understand if you can't forgive me.'

His face broke into a broad smile, and he threw back his head. 'Yes,' he cried out to the sky above. 'Oh, yes!' And he reached out to her and pulled her close to him. 'I could never hate you, Jenny – I love you far too much for that.' And he wrapped his arms around her and buried his face in her hair.

'Despite everything?' she asked, her voice muffled by the T-shirt she was being crushed against.

'Definitely despite everything.' His arms tightened around her. 'This morning's been sheer hell. I thought I might have lost you for ever, and I never want to feel that way again. The houses, the paintings, my company – nothing means anything if you can't share it with the person you love. From the moment I met you, *you* have been the person I love. Without you, my life would be empty.'

She pulled slightly back and gazed up at him in naked relief. 'Oh, Max, when you left, I was so unhappy. I thought you wouldn't want me any more.'

'Not want you?' He stared down into her face with a passion that took her breath away. 'I shall always want you. You say that you can't bear to think of life without me, well I know that I can't bear to think of life without you. And that means there's only one thing for it. Will you marry me?'

'Oh, yes, I will,' she cried. 'I love you, I love you, I love you. Now that I can finally say it, I feel so free. And so very, very happy. I don't deserve to be this happy.'

'Yes, you do.' He lifted his hand and lightly traced the arch of her brow, the line of her nose, the fullness of her lips, the curve of her chin. Then he took her face in his hands and looked down at her.

'I've many beautiful pictures at home in England,' he said, his voice full of wonder, 'and I've many beautiful pictures here, but nothing comes close to how beautiful you are to me. You're a picture that I'll never tire of looking at, and I shall be the luckiest person alive if I'm able to do so every day for the rest of my life.'

A low sigh of sheer bliss escaped her, and she raised herself on her toes, brought her lips to his and silenced him.

About the Author

Liz was born in London and now lives in South Oxfordshire with her husband. After graduating from university with a Law degree, she moved to California where she led a varied life, trying her hand at everything from cocktail waitressing on Sunset Strip to working as a secretary to the CEO of a large Japanese trading company, not to mention a stint as 'resident starlet' at MGM. On returning to England, Liz completed a degree in English and taught for a number of years before developing her writing career.

Liz has written several short stories, articles for local newspapers and novellas. She is a member of the Romantic Novelists' Association. *The Road Back* won a Book of the Year Award. Her second novel *A Bargain Struck* was shortlisted for the Romantic Historical Novel of the Year Award.

Follow Liz on:
Twitter @lizharrisauthor
Facebook: https://www.facebook.com/liz.harris.52206
Web: www.lizharrisauthor.com

More Choc Lit

From Liz Harris

The Road Back

Winner of the 2012 Book of the Year Award from Coffee Time Romance & More

When Patricia accompanies her father, Major George Carstairs, on a trip to Ladakh, north of the Himalayas, in the early 1960s, she sees it as a chance to finally win his love. What she could never have foreseen is meeting Kalden – a local man destined by circumstances beyond his control to be a monk, but fated to be the love of her life.

'A splendid love story so beautifully told.' Colin Dexter, O.B.E. Bestselling author of the Inspector Morse series.

A Bargain Struck

Book 1 in the Heart of the West Series

Shortlisted for the 2014 Romantic Historical Novel of the Year Award

Does a good deal make a marriage?
Widower Connor Maguire advertises for a wife to raise his young daughter, Bridget, work the homestead and bear him a son. Ellen O'Sullivan longs for a home, a husband and a family. On paper, she is everything Connor needs in a wife.

As their personal feelings blur the boundaries of their deal, they begin to wonder if a bargain struck makes a marriage worth keeping.

Set in Wyoming in 1887, a story of a man and a woman brought together through need, not love ...